Frances E. Cooke

An American Hero

The Story of William Lloyd Garrison

Frances E. Cooke

An American Hero
The Story of William Lloyd Garrison

ISBN/EAN: 9783337191955

Printed in Europe, USA, Canada, Australia, Japan

Cover: Foto ©Raphael Reischuk / pixelio.de

More available books at **www.hansebooks.com**

AN AMERICAN HERO

THE STORY OF WILLIAM LLOYD GARRISON

Written for Young People

BY

FRANCES E. COOKE

*Author of "An English Hero," "William Tyndale's Vow," "Noble Workers,"
Etc.*

"O SMALL beginnings, ye are great and strong,
Based on a faithful heart and weariless brain,
Ye build the future fair, ye conquer wrong."

LOWELL

LONDON

GEORGE ROUTLEDGE & SONS, LIMITED

BROADWAY HOUSE, CARTER LANE, E.C.

CONTENTS.

CHAPTER VII.

CHAPTER VIII.

CHAPTER IX.

CHAPTER X.

CHAPTER XI.

AN AMERICAN HERO.

CHAPTER I.

NEWBURYPORT.

ONE spring day in the year 1805, a ship from Nova Scotia anchored in the harbour of Newburyport, Massachusetts. A sea-captain named Abijah Garrison was among her passengers. Hard times had driven him from his old home in the North, and he had come with his wife and their two little children to seek a living in the United States. The first sight of Newburyport was cheering after their long voyage. The town was built on the side of a hill: at the foot lay ship-yards and wharves filled with merchant vessels and fishing boats, and breezes from the Atlantic Ocean brought health and strength to the dwellers in the busy seaport. Among the streets and houses were still to be seen patches of meadow-land and groups of shady trees, remnants of country life, pleasant and restful to the eye.

When the new settlers landed, their first business was to find a home; and their search ended in a wooden house in School Street, where they rented from Martha Farnham, the wife of a coasting captain, some rooms that she did not need for her own use. One end of the dwelling, which from this time held two families, was joined to a chapel; at the other end lay a little garden. There were five windows above, and two at each side, of the narrow doorway; and in front ran the public highway, busy with the traffic of foot-passengers and heavily laden wains, sheltered at intervals with well-grown chestnut-trees.

In this house, on December 10th, 1805, a new baby was added to the Garrison family, and the names William Lloyd were given to him—the latter being his mother's maiden name. Within a short time other changes took place : the little daughter, who had been brought from Nova Scotia, died, and when Lloyd was three years

old, another little sister, whom they named
Maria Elizabeth, was born. Then there were
three children in the home—two boys and a girl.
The clever captain, soon after his arrival in
Newburyport, had found a post in one of the
many ships belonging to the town; and all
might have gone well with him if his moral
courage had been equal to his physical valour.
But many of the sailors, his new companions,
were intemperate men; and though he feared
no storms on the Atlantic Ocean, he was not
brave enough to say " No " when they tempted
him to drink. Matters grew worse and worse
as time went on, and, in less than four years
from the day when they landed in Newburyport, Captain Garrison forsook his wife and
children, and never came back to them again.

So troubles came early to little Lloyd
Garrison. Before he was seven years old, he
shared his mother's cares. Every penny gained
was of importance, and the little lad was sent
out to sell sticks of candy in the town. Many
a good-natured passer-by bought his wares,
struck by the child's eager face : and after such
good fortune, Lloyd used to run home joyfully
with the money he had earned. Sometimes he

was sent with a can to a large house in State
Street for soup and bread which his mother
was thankful to receive. At such times, small
as he was, the boy used to shrink from the
sight of other children as he carried his can,
yet he hardly recognised himself the feeling
which made him anxious to work rather than
to live on charity.

Good Mrs. Farnham was very kind to the
poor mother and children whom she had taken
into her house. And when, in course of time,
Mrs. Garrison found employment as nurse in
the town of Llyn, it was a great trouble to her
to be obliged to leave the home which had
sheltered her for so many years. Her eldest
boy, James, she took with her; the little
daughter, Elizabeth, she left in Mrs. Farnham's
care, and Lloyd, at seven years of age, found
himself in a new home.

At the foot of the hill on which Newburyport was built, near the busy ship-yards, lived
old Deacon Bartlett and his wife. They were
friends of Mrs. Garrison's, and members of the
Baptist Church in which she used to worship.
They were quite poor people. Close to their
door they kept a little apple-stand, where they

sold fruit to thirsty sailors on hot summer days.
Behind the house was a wood-yard, where the
deacon sawed planks and made up bundles of
chips for sale. There Lloyd went to live. His
school-days were few, and the ways of learning
were by no means pleasant ways for him. He
was left-handed, and the stern schoolmaster
rapped his knuckles, and had little patience with
his efforts to learn to write. So he was much
happier when splitting wood with the deacon,
or carrying out chips to customers in the town.
Yet he worked hard at school, and though his
school hours were fewer, and his difficulties
greater, than those of his school-fellows, he
learned to write a better hand than any of
them. On Sundays, he sang in the choir of the
Baptist Church, and people who listened with
delight to his clear, flute-like voice, saw with
surprise that the little chorister was the bare-
footed boy who sold them their firewood during
the week.

The breezy streets and open common of
Newburyport were fine playgrounds for Lloyd
when his work was done. There he rolled his
hoop and ran races with companions as full
of spirit as himself. But dearest of all haunts

was the river Merrimac, which flowed within a
stone's-throw of the deacon's door. He learned
to swim like a fish in its waters, to scull in the
good-natured seamen's boats, and in the winter
to slide and skate. He was like an untrained
colt in those days, and now and then got into
mischief; but he was always honest and true
and tender-hearted, and though eager for fun,
Lloyd was faithful to the old deacon who had
to work so hard for a living, and he never forsook the apple-stall or the chip-yard when his
work was wanted, though the Merrimac lay
sparkling in the sunlight, and he could hear
his comrade's voices as they shouted at their
play.

Meanwhile, Lloyd's mother still lived at Llyn.
The boy loved her heartily, and prized her
letters, and wrote to her in return. He would
have done anything to please her; his greatest
wish, small as he was, was to learn a trade, so
that he might in time support her in comfort.
So at nine years of age, the little fellow was
ready when she sent for him to Llyn to learn
shoe-making. The heavy lapstone wearied
him, the strong waxed thread hurt his fingers,
and the workmen laughed at him and told him

he was "no bigger than a last." But he was brave and persevering, and proud of his success when in some months' time he had made his first shoe.

Then came a change. The shoemaker failed, and Lloyd was apprenticed to a cabinet-maker in another town, away from his mother, and also from his old friends at Newburyport. Then he grew homesick and longed for the old deacon, and a sight of the sparkling Merrimac, and a breath of the fresh winds that blew from the Atlantic over his native town. His work pleased his master, who treated him kindly; but one summer morning, the young apprentice could bear his loneliness no longer, and set off over hill and dale, with his bundle over his shoulder, to walk to Newburyport and find fresh work among his old friends. He was overtaken and had to go back with the cabinet-maker and talk over his plans, which he ought to have done before. But when all was made plain, his master parted from him in a friendly manner, and Lloyd set forth again for Newburyport, a boy of only fourteen years of age, with his own way to make in the world.

The tradesmen of Newburyport became used

to the sight of the honest-faced lad who
sought so eagerly all that summer for work.
The breezy common and sunny Merrimac were
seldom play-places for him now : for deep down
in his loving heart lay the firm resolve to be a
comfort to his mother, and to be that, he must
find some work to do.   So it was a happy day
for him when Mr. Allen, the editor of the
Newburyport Herald, agreed to take him as his
apprentice; and on October 18th, 1818, Lloyd
entered his printing office to learn the printer's
trade.   Still, there were difficulties before him,
and this was well, for Lloyd Garrison had not
only to earn a livelihood, but to build up a
character.   It seemed to him at first hopeless
that he should ever learn to set type rapidly.
He felt clumsy and slow, and was not even tall
enough to reach the table at which he. had to
work.   How far away seemed the hope of
making a home for his mother !   The young
apprentice earned little more than his board
and clothes.   It was no easy matter to pay for
the postage of his letters to her; yet he wrote
often, for it was the only pleasure he could give
to his mother and the little sister, who was now
living with her.   Mrs. Garrison's health had

broken down. She could no longer work; but happily she had found kind friends to help her. In her poverty and pain she was cheered by the news of her brave boy as the weeks went by and he was able to tell her of the progress he had made in learning the work of the printing office.

Lloyd's new home was in the printer's house which was near that of his old friend, Deacon Bartlett, and he soon made friends in the printer's wife and children. His master trusted and liked him and his willing, ready ways. As he grew more experienced in setting type, he was able to read and to think as he set it, and thus his place of work became as school and college to him. He borrowed books and formed opinions about the politics of Newburyport. At length he took a new and daring step. Evening after evening the printer's children wondered what made Lloyd so busy that he had no time to devote to them when working hours were over. They would have wondered still more if they had seen his excited, hopeful face when, one night, he dropped a packet into the post-office, and ran home whistling to await the result. The fact was, Lloyd had ventured to write in a disguised hand an article for the *Newburyport Herald*, of which his master was the editor ; and when next morning Mr. Allen received the packet, and, having read its contents, handed the article to Lloyd to put in type for the newspaper, there was no happier young printer in the United States. He sent other papers after this which were also accepted, and only to his mother did Lloyd tell of this new interest in his life. He had still better news to send her when his master, called away on business, trusted him so far as to leave him, still only an apprentice, in charge of the printing office during his absence. After this came a holiday spent in a visit to his mother. Mrs. Garrison had not seen her boy for seven years, and it was the greatest comfort to her to find him as tender and faithful as he was strong. This proved to be the last time the mother and son were to meet on earth. In less than three months afterwards Lloyd heard of her death. His little sister had passed away before her, and nothing had been heard for a long time of his brother James who had gone to sea, so now Lloyd was the only remaining member of the family. There was a dreary blank in the boy's

life : the motive for his work was lost; there
was now no mother for whom he must make a
home ; but the memory of her brave, unselfish
life never left him, and in after years the
thought of what she had wished him to become
acted as a powerful influence over him.

For nearly three years after his mother's
death, Lloyd worked on in Mr. Allen's printing
office. No youth in Newburyport was more
worthy of trust than he, and any task which he
undertook was always faithfully performed.
He was strong and quick and active, and the
fierce winds which blew over Newburyport
and lashed the waters of the Merrimac into
frequent storm, tended to make him brave and
fearless of hardships. It was a good training
for the stirring life that lay before him. Newburyport was wide awake in politics. There
was a strong Liberal party in the town not
afraid of change and progress, and Lloyd
Garrison threw in his lot with such men. Away
in Europe the Greeks were fighting for freedom
from Turkish rule, and his boyish sympathies
were roused by the news of their struggle. He
even longed to go and help them, and use his
strong right arm in their cause. Perhaps it

sometimes seemed to him less heroic to be
setting type in a dull newspaper office than to
march to battle against tyrants to defend oppressed men and women. But, however that
might be, his type was always well set, and he
was the most rapid and correct compositor in
Mr. Allen's printing works. There was better
work in store for Lloyd Garrison than mere
force of weapons could achieve, and meanwhile,
like many another hero, he was making ready
for the day when God would call him to it.

Lloyd Garrison was a pleasant companion as
well as a hard worker, and many of the young
people of Newburyport liked him well. But
there were few among them whom he could
choose for *friends*. Life was an earnest matter
to him, and he cared most for those who were
in earnest, and who sought after what was true
and lasting. Isaac Knapp was such an one—a
youth who, like himself, had made his own way
in the world. Often the two lads talked together of work they hoped to do before they
died, and they planned great and noble schemes,
such as boys often set before themselves, but
too often forget like idle dreams as the years
pass by. There was a quiet room over a book-

THE OLD GRAMMAR SCHOOL, NEWBURYPORT.
GARRISON'S BIRTHPLACE.

[Face p. 12.

store in the town where the two friends were
welcome in the evenings to meet and read
together, and talk over what they had read. In
this book-store, William Crocker, a youth a few
months older than Lloyd Garrison, was an
apprentice. He had been a shoemaker, and
before many years were over, he was to go out
as a missionary into distant lands where at last
he died in his self-chosen banishment. He, too,
was in earnest, and was another of Lloyd's
favourite companions. So months passed by,
and the three friends grew up towards manhood. Lloyd ended his apprenticeship, and in
the early days of 1826 he said good-bye to the
Herald office, and set on foot a paper of his
own, which he called the *Free Press.* He had
no money for such a venture ; but Mr. Allen
knew by that time of what stuff his old apprentice was made, and lent him the sum he
needed, knowing well that the debt would be
paid in due time. And now the little bare-
footed boy who had carried the old deacon's
chips from door to door, was an editor and
publisher in Newburyport.

CHAPTER II

CHOOSING A SIDE.

HILE Lloyd Garrison was thus growing up to manhood in Newburyport, a farmer's son named John Greenleaf Whittier was spending his boyhood in the pleasant country at Haverhill eighteen miles further up the river Merrimac. There, among sheltering woods and broad meadows, stood old farmsteads that had been in the possession of the same families for years past. Their owners knew and cared little about the busy world beyond their own blue hills. Squirrels and wild birds made their nests in that quiet country where there was no man to make them afraid, and healthy, happy children played on the river banks and grew up to work on the old farms as their fathers before them had done.

Such an old homestead was owned by the Quaker, Farmer Whittier. He and his family had no need to go beyond the borders of their own farm for the means of living. Their sheep and flax provided wool and linen for their homespun clothes. The mother and daughters spun and kept the house, and the father and his boys worked on the farm—a quiet, uneventful life. The Quaker meeting-house was too far away for more than a rare visit, and the children saw no faces except those of the neighbours who owned the other farms at Haverhill—with one exception. An old Scotchman used to come round sometimes with his pack on his back selling small wares to the farmers' wives: and it was a great event when he hung up his plaid and stayed for a night's shelter under the kind-hearted Quaker's roof. To please the children, he used to sing to them old Scotch ballads; and after one visit, he left behind him a volume of Burns' poems for the boy to read, whose eager, happy face he had watched during the singing of the songs. This boy was John Greenleaf Whittier, who must now appear in Lloyd Garrison's story.

Dressed in home-spun clothes, ploughing and

digging all the summer-time like the other
young farmers of Haverhill, no one suspected
that John Whittier had any other thoughts and
dreams beyond those that satisfied their lives.
But the fact was that as he went about his
work, everything he saw spoke to him of
some hidden beauty. The brook which flowed
through his father's garden, the wild flowers
in the meadows, the distant mountains, and all
the other country sights and sounds—all these
pictures took shape in musical words, and
floated through his mind as he guided the
plough or drove the cattle home from pasture
in the evening.

But writing poetry seemed nothing but folly
to the good old Quaker farmer; and since, if
John did his work well, he might spend his
leisure as he chose, tho boy wrote out these
poems, which came to him he knew not whence,
and he kept a little store of them hidden away
behind the rubbish in an unused garret of the
old farmhouse.

Time passed, and Lloyd Garrison, at Newburyport, down the river Merrimac, finished
his apprenticeship, and set on foot his own
paper, the *Free Press.* Some numbers reached

Haverhill. Farmer Whittier read them, and was struck with the honest, straightforward tone of the editor's leading articles. So a breath of fresh air from the outside world entered the old farmhouse every week from the day when the carrier began to bring the *Free Press* from Newburyport, and throw it over the Whittiers' garden fence. Now in the paper there was a " Poet's Corner," for Lloyd Garrison had a high ideal for his news-paper. He wished not only to give his readers right views on politics, and to discuss fairly the great questions of the day; but also to give them noble and beautiful thoughts to read, and the young poet-farmer at Haverhill began to look forward eagerly to the arrival of the *Free Press*, for the sake of the poems that were inserted in it.

One day John Whittier was mending the fence, when the carrier from Newburyport stopped his horse in the road to throw him the paper. What was the boy's surprise to find a poem of his own, called the " Exile's Departure," in the much-prized " Poet's Corner." There it stood in clear print signed " W," and beneath it a note from the editor,

C

asking for more poems from the same writer ! What magic had brought about this strange event? It was soon explained. His sister, far prouder of John's success than ever he himself would be, had found his secret store of poems in the old garret, and had ventured to send one of them, written out with trembling fingers and a beating heart, to the office of the *Free Press*.

And how had Lloyd Garrison received the poem ? The pale ink was very hard to read, and his first impulse was to tear up the " original poem," which was little likely to be of any use to him. But the writing was in an unformed, youthful hand, and perhaps at the sight there came across his mind the memory of the day when he had sent his first paper to the *Newburyport Herald* and his good friend, Mr. Allen, had given him courage to persevere. So he read it through and then he found that his youthful correspondent gave promise of great future power. Other poems followed. As he read them, Lloyd began to wish to know their author's name. At last he learned that his poet was a boy hard at work in the fields at Haverhill.

The young editor resolved that he would
seek out this youth who probably needed help
in the struggle of life ; and one summer day,
when the *Free Press* was still only six
months old, he took a holiday and drove out
from Newburyport along the pleasant country
roads to Haverhill. As has been said, it was
a rare event for any stranger to visit Mr.
Whittier's farm ; and when the new-comer from
the distant town accosted the old Quaker,
saying, " I want to see you about your son,"
the farmer asked, somewhat anxiously, " What
has the boy been doing ? "

Meanwhile, John was at work in the field
bare-footed, and his sister was sent to summon
him to the stranger's presence. In came the
farm-boy, waiting only to put on his jacket and
shoes, timid, yet eager to see the great man,
whose errand, no doubt, the loving sister had
partly guessed. He found a youth hardly older
than himself talking to his father, and advising
him to give an education to the lad who could
write unaided such poems as the *Free Press*
had printed.

" Poetry will never give him bread," said the
straightforward Quaker, who objected to having

"such notions put in the boy's head." But Lloyd Garrison's sympathy had wakened to new life the slumbering energies within the young farmer's mind. "Where there's a will, there's a way." All through that summer and the following autumn, John worked well on the farm, and no day-dreams nor poet's fancies interfered with the duties that fell to his lot. Then came winter, bringing long months when the snow lay on the ground and no farm-work could be done. John spent his leisure in learning to make shoes from a labourer on his father's farm who was willing to teach him his winter's trade, and by this occupation he earned enough to buy a suit of clothes in the spring, and to pay for a term's study at the Haverhill Academy; for Lloyd Garrison still stood his friend, and prevailed on the farmer to agree to the boy's great longing.

But before that term was ended, Lloyd's own fortunes had changed. The *Free Press* had proved to be too outspoken for the people of Newburyport. Its brave young editor would not write to please the public. Men found in its pages fearless words about right and wrong that somewhat roughly handled their

own hobbies, and after a fair trial, it was plain
that the paper would not pay. It was rather
hard to go back as a journeyman printer to his
old master's office; but Lloyd Garrison had
a brave heart, and no difficulties damped his
courage; so for three months he set type there
as he had done when a boy. Then, when all
the affairs of the *Free Press* were settled, and
the loan from Mr. Allen repaid, he set forth to
Boston to begin the world afresh, with no money
and no friends in the unknown town. A printer
who knew the character he had borne in Newburyport gave him a home in his house till he
could earn money to pay for his board; but there
were hard times just then in Boston, and many
men were out of work. Lloyd had a long and
weary search. Day after day he visited offices,
to be met by the same answer that there was
no room for him. Yet there was an impulse
within him which bore him bravely on. His
mind was not only fixed on bread-winning. He
saw that there was great work to be done in
the world, and great need of workers, right
causes to be helped and wrongs to be redressed,
and he was eager to be a helper on the right
side. So each morning he went forth with

fresh zeal to seek a little niche in which he
might plant himself among the world's workers.

And at length he found it.

There was a paper published in Boston called
the *National Philanthropist*. So far it had
scarcely paid its way, and a pushing editor was
needed to help it forward. The post was
offered to Lloyd Garrison, and he gladly took
it; for it promised to give him not only the
means of living, but also the means of influence
he wished for. It was the first temperance
paper ever published, and was greatly needed
in those days, when drinking customs were so
widely spread. Lloyd widened its use, and
made it the organ of other reforms; and the
citizens of Boston found there, beside their
daily news, honesty in politics, and brave words
against the sins and follies of society in their
town.

While Lloyd was still searching for work, a
great meeting was held in Boston, to consider
the choice of a representative to Congress.
The nomination was at hand, and young Garrison felt very strongly that a wrong man was
likely to be chosen. It was true that he himself was young in years and unknown to his

fellow-citizens, and doubtless he shrank from
the ordeal of his first public speech. Neverthe-
less, he was in earnest, and must bring all the
influence he could to support the right. There
was a stirring among the excited people, and
a cry of "Who is he?" when this youthful
stranger mounted on a bench and laid before
the crowd the higher grounds which should
rule their votes, and which he thought they
failed to see. He broke down before the close
of his speech; but his words prevailed, and the
justice and truth deep down within his hearers
rose up in answer, and public opinion was
changed by the brave, honest speech of a young
man friendless and out of work. This promised well for his usefulness in after years.
But too often the fair promises of youth fade
away and are forgotten. Was it to be so in
his case? We shall see.

Very often, during his life in Boston, Lloyd's
thoughts went back to the happy evenings at
Newburyport, when he and his friend Isaac
Knapp had read together, and talked over the
questions which they had found hard to solve
in these early days. Glad would he have been
of this lost companion now, as he thought

about the great matters which were stirring the
minds of men, and which he could not leave
unnoticed in the pages of his paper. He used
to take long solitary walks on Boston Common,
away from the noises of the town, that the fresh
breezes which blew over it might help to clear
his weary brain; and one day, while the winter
snow was lying thickly, and stormy winds were
blowing, in the first week of the year 1828, he
sought its silence and solitude to consider a
new problem. Was it just and right, he asked
himself, that a bill should be passed in one of
the Southern States, forbidding coloured men
and women to learn to read and write? Such
was the question to which he must find an
answer; for such a bill had just been passed
in South Carolina, and the *National Philanthropist* must not pass the news over in silence.
Surely there must be something wrong in the
system that led masters, for the sake of their
own safety, to seal up the inquiring minds of
their slaves, and keep them on the level of the
brutes. As he pondered, a clear light began to
dawn on Lloyd Garrison's mind, and he went
on to question, for the first time, whether
negro slavery, which was established by law

in the Southern States of America was not a
crime.

Boston citizens who read the *Philanthropist*
that week were startled by the bold opinions
which the little paper put forth against the
scheme of the South Carolina Bill. It was a
new thing to see the rights of the slaves defended, and to see them spoken of as human
beings, instead of chattels to be bought and
sold. But the surprise ended with the week,
and the subject was dropped again in Boston;
for there, as in all other cities in the Northern
States, it was a dangerous matter to utter a
whisper against the slavery of the South, which
brought the North its wealth. Boston was the
great market for slave-grown cotton. There
merchants lived who made their money by
cotton traffic. On slave labour depended the
prosperity of the North; and to question the
white man's right to enslave the negroes would
be to endanger the Union itself. So all Boston
believed, and on all sides there was silence
about the great national sin. But Lloyd Garrison could not stifle the promptings of his
conscience, and every day his belief grew
stronger that the slave system was wrong.

About this time a stranger to Boston, named Benjamin Lundy, came to the printer's house, where Lloyd was living, and asked for a few nights' lodging. He was already known by name to young Garrison, who, when he was a boy, had heard Mr. Lundy's eventful story, and thought of him as a hero. Lloyd had pictured to himself a very different person from the small, insignificant-looking deaf man who now stood before him; and no one will wonder at this who reads the tale of Lundy's brave life. He was born a Quaker in the State of New Jersey, which borders on Massachusetts; and while Lloyd Garrison was still a baby in Mrs. Farnham's little wooden house in Newburyport, the young Quaker had gone out into the world to earn a living. And he had wandered in search of it southwards, till in the slave-holding State of Virginia he had found a saddler at Wheeling, on the river Ohio, who took him as an apprentice, and promised to teach him his trade. The New Jersey boy was honest and hard-working, and he prospered in his new home as time went on. When his apprenticeship was at an end, he set up in business as a saddler. His work was so good that he soon

found custom, married, and made a home, and
all would have gone well and happily with him
had not his tender heart been touched by the
constant sight of sorrows he could not relieve;
for in those days, gangs of slaves used to be
driven chained together through the streets of
Wheeling, on their way down the river to hopeless slavery in States still further south. The
sight of their sad faces, and the sound of the
cruel driver's lash, filled him with a longing to
help them; and he resolved, when in a few
years he had made some money, to sell his
saddler's business, and set on foot a newspaper
that might draw attention to their woes. He
knew nothing about printing, and at first walked
twenty miles each week to get his paper printed,
bringing back the edition in a pack on his
shoulders, and selling copies as he went on his
way. By-and-by he bought a press of his
own, and learned to use it; but his wandering
life still continued. He travelled on foot from
State to State, holding meetings in various
towns, and telling everywhere the same tale of
the sufferings of the slaves. Meanwhile he lost
thousands of dollars; and at last a very poor
man, with no capital of his own, he removed to

Baltimore, and there published a paper called
the *Genius of Universal Emancipation.* There
his wife, whom he loved dearly, died, his children were scattered, and his home was broken
up. Pity for the slaves, whose sorrows were
so much greater than his own, made him forget
his losses in still harder work for them; and
years passed away in such self-sacrificing
labour.

No wonder Lloyd Garrison was ready to
greet a hero when for the first time he met
this man. The poor Quaker, on his side, bent
and worn with anxiety and overwork, saw in
the strong youth, so full of energy, and eager
to stand by the right, the promise of a noble
worker in years to come. They had much talk
together, and Lloyd entered heartily into the
plan when Mr. Lundy told him that he had
invited all the clergymen in Boston to meet
him, that they might form an anti-slavery society
in the city. When the day appointed for the
meeting came, the unwearied man waited the
result of his invitations. Lloyd Garrison hoped
for the best, and waited with him. Boston was
already rich in good works, and there were
famous preachers in her churches. Might it

not be that this brave man would succeed in
rousing them to consider the long-neglected
question? The doubt was soon ended. One
by one the clergymen dropped in. Only eight
came; yet how much might not *eight* wise men
do if they were in earnest. Benjamin Lundy
rose to speak, and his bent form and feeble
voice were soon forgotten in the enthusiasm
of his words, as he told his mission to Boston.

Years afterwards, Lloyd Garrison recalled the
story of that meeting in these words:—" He
might as well have urged the stones in the
street to cry out on behalf of the perishing
captives. My soul was on fire. Every soul in
the room was heartily opposed to slavery, *but*—
but it would terribly alarm and enrage the
South to know that an anti-slavery society
existed in Boston. *But*—it would do harm
rather than good to agitate the subject; *but*—
we had nothing to do with the subject, and
the less we meddled with it, the better. Oh!
the moral cowardice, the chilling apathy, the
criminal unbelief, the cruel scepticism that were
revealed on that memorable occasion! Poor
Lundy! that meeting was a damper to his

feelings; but he was not a man to be cast down, come what might."

So ended Benjamin Lundy's mission to Boston, and the following day he set forth to sow his seed in less stony ground. Garrison carried about with him the memory of the noble, homeless man, and thought how sadly Boston needed heroes like him, who were ready to uphold the right at all costs. For four months longer he edited the *Philanthropist*. At the end of that time the paper fell into the hands of fresh owners, and he had to consider what should be his next step in life.

CHAPTER III.

 GREAT event was at hand in the United States, and the whole nation was excited and astir. Towards the end of the year a new President was to be elected, and even villages and country towns far away from the seat of Government at Washington forgot their local politics and lesser interests in view of the great national struggle. In the farthest corner of Vermont, under the shadow of the Green Mountains, the village of Bennington was wide awake to the claims of the rival candidates, and there came thence a little company of men seeking Lloyd Garrison at Boston, with the request that he would take up his abode among them in the distant Vermont village, and become the edi-

tor of a new paper which should uphold the election of John Quincy Adams, the present President, whose term of office was drawing to a close.

Now Garrison was quite ready to uphold the claims of Mr. Adams, and the object of the journal had his full sympathy. But he was not willing to spend his time and strength in the pursuit of politics alone, while there were so many great moral evils to be mended in the world, and he could raise his voice against them. So he made answer that he would accept the post they offered him on one condition: and this was, that he might be free to deal in the paper as he liked with the great questions of war and slavery and intemperance; and to this condition the "citizens" of Bennington agreed.

The new paper was to be called the *Journal of the Times*, and the first number was to appear in October. In the interval, Lloyd went to see his friends in Newburyport. He met with a hearty welcome from Mr. Allen, the printer, and renewed the old intercourse with his friend Isaac Knapp. What a pleasure it was to revisit, after his absence, the places where his boyhood had been spent : the little wooden house in School Street, where good Mrs. Farnham had been a kind friend to his mother in her trouble ; the chapel where he had sung on Sundays, and the woodyard where he had worked with the old deacon. As he wandered by the Merrimac, he seemed to hear again the voices of his old companions, with whom he had had such merry times when he was only a little bare-footed errand-boy ; and as he went up and down the hilly streets, memories came back to him of his weary search for work so many years ago, when, homesick and lonely, he had made his way back from the cabinet-maker's employment to his native town.

The summer was over when he reached his new home in Vermont. The woods were rich with golden autumn tints, and there was beauty on every side. The clear blue sky by day and the bright starlight nights were a constant delight to him. Before his printing-office door lay the village green, where the men of Bennington used to meet when their day's work was over, to discuss the events of the day, and the news from foreign lands. He found them frank, hard-working people, ready to

D

welcome new ideas, and there were six hundred
subscribers to his paper in the first week.

Bennington lay in a valley running north and
south. Full in view in the east rose the Green
Mountains with cloud shadows chasing the
sunlight over their slopes, and in the west the
grand heights of Mount Anthony stood up dark
and purple against the sunset skies. In the
midst of so much outward beauty, grand ideals
seemed to rise before the youth's mind with
greater clearness than of old, and great questions of right and wrong grew more plain to
his judgment, and stronger than ever grew his
longing to do some good work in the world,
and help to mend some crooked ways before
he died. The *Journal of the Times* gained
supporters for Mr. Adams, and the political
leaders in the paper were all that were
required. But its usefulness did not end there:
Lloyd Garrison's words in the new journal
roused his hearers to think on whatever subject
he wrote, for they came straight from his heart.
So, on the village green at Bennington that
autumn, topics were discussed that had been
passed over in silence hitherto; and wherever
the *Journal of the Times* made its way, men

could not close their ears to such a trumpet-call
as the following, which appeared in its pages:—

"It is time that a remonstrance went forth
from the North that should peal in the ear of
every slave-holder like the roar of thunder.
For ourselves, we are resolved to agitate this
subject to the utmost. Nothing but death
shall prevent us from denouncing a crime
which has no parallel in human depravity.
We shall take high ground. The alarm must
be perpetual."

Prudent and cautious people, when they read
the *Journal of the Times*, shook their heads
over such bold handling of an unsafe theme.
But there were no slave-holders in Vermont,
and it was a far cry from there to Boston,
where the cotton trade brought men their daily
bread. So the outspoken young editor was
allowed to take his own course ; and it was said
that the novelty of its contents helped the sale
of the journal. None of these considerations
weighed with Lloyd Garrison, however. All he
knew was that he could not keep silence in face
of such an evil. But words of sympathy helped
to give him courage, and a few of these reached
him sometimes.

John Greenleaf Whittier, the farmer's son at Haverhill, whom he had befriended three years before, had shown himself worthy of the help then given him; and while still working patiently at the cobbler's bench, and on his father's farm, had toiled eagerly up the hard ways of learning. And Lloyd Garrison had never lost sight of him; had published his poems in his Boston paper, and had written cheering words to him. No wonder that the youth never forgot that summer morning when, in the old farmhouse, Garrison's words to his father had changed the whole current of his unsatisfied life. No wonder that he loved Lloyd Garrison with boyish enthusiasm. As he read the *Journal of the Times*, he saw in Garrison's writing the prophecy of a great career, and he ventured to write a letter to him, urging him to be of good courage, and to labour bravely on against slavery, in the certain hope that there were great things waiting for him to do. And this letter gladdened Garrison when he read it.

Far away in Baltimore, Benjamin Lundy was watching whether the hopes he had formed of the young printer, whom he had met in Boston, were to be realized. Month after month, tokens reached him that young Garrison's whole soul was against the sin of slavery; and at last he resolved to carry out a scheme which became dearer to him every day. He would go to Bennington, and try to induce the fearless youth to come to Baltimore, in the heart of the slave States, and help him to put new life into his anti-slavery paper, *The Genius.* So the good Quaker, too poor to make the long journey, except on foot, took his pack on his back, and his staff in his hand, and set forth over hill and dale to the Green Mountains in Vermont. Thick snow lay on the ground, and chill winds and cutting hailstorms blew and beat against him as he went day after day on his dreary journey. But no obstacles nor hardships daunted him; and when he came in sight of the great hills that sheltered Bennington, he forgot his weariness in his longing to grasp Garrison's friendly hand once more, and gain the promise of his much-needed help.

The two men took solemn counsel together. It was no light matter for Garrison to agree to the step the older man urged him to take. His proposal was that the *Genius* should be pub-

ished once a week, instead of once a month;
and while Garrison lived in Baltimore and took
charge of the paper, Lundy was to travel and
find fresh subscribers. Lloyd had now been
six months at Bennington. The President's
election was over: General Jackson, a slave-
holder, had been elected; so all the efforts of
the *Journal of the Times* to oppose him had
been in vain. As he thought over the new
scheme proposed to him, Lloyd saw that it
opened a wider field of usefulness before him;
his task in Bennington was done, and he agreed
to leave his Vermont home at the end of March,
1829, and follow Benjamin Lundy to the new
and dangerous task.

During his long journey, Lloyd had time to
meditate on all that lay before him. He was
going to the home of slave-owners. At Baltimore, slaves torn from their friends were sold
or shipped to Southern markets. Yet there,
in the midst of resolute slave-traders, he was
to raise the warning cry that slavery was a
sin, and must end. What would be his fate?
Hitherto the gentle voice of Lundy had hardly
been noticed. The end and aim of the *Genius*
had been the *gradual* emancipation of the

slaves; and though it told of the pains and sorrows they endured, the indefinite future when
they should gain their freedom had no terror
for the slave-owners. But Garrison knew that
this mode of treatment must end now. Slavery
was wrong, and, like all other wrongs, must be
put an end to *at once.* Men made excuses and
silenced the voice of conscience. Now he
would speak, and they *should* listen, whatever
might be the result to himself. That was in
God's hands, and he had to think of nothing
but his duty. And this was a penniless youth
of twenty-four years old!

As soon as he reached Baltimore, Lloyd told
Mr. Lundy what he had resolved to do. But
it was like yoking a lion to a lamb to make
partners of these two men, and the gentle,
timid Quaker shrank back from the young
man's daring. He ended their talk thus:
"Thou shalt put thy initials to thy articles,
and I will put my initials to my articles, and
each of us will bear his own burden." "Very
good," replied Lloyd Garrison; "that will
answer, and I shall be able to free my soul."

Then the partners began their work. Mr.
Lundy set forth on his travels. Lloyd Garrison

lived in Baltimore, and edited the weekly issue
of the *Genius*. Day by day he saw the weep-
ing slaves driven, chained together, through
the city streets, on their way to the river Ohio,
to embark to Southern towns. He heard the
slave-driver's whip and the bitter cry. News
came to Baltimore that a plan was on foot to
wrest the great free lands of Texas from
Mexico, and make fresh slave states there.
When Lloyd Garrison heard this, he cried :
" What sort of religion have these men ?
There is no courage in the land and no faith-
fulness." The former gentle whisper of the
Genius changed to a voice of thunder, and the
slave-holders of Baltimore and the region
round about listened, and their anger knew no
bounds. They muttered threats against Garrison, and were fiercely indignant at the pro-
posals he made. " It would be dangerous to
free the slaves," they cried ; " they would rise
up and cut their old masters' throats." In
Northern cities copies of the *Genius* were read,
and there the cry was, " The North will be
ruined—the Union will be broken. That mad-
cap Garrison must be silenced ! " After this,
subscriptions to the paper began to fall off.

Where Lundy got one subscriber, Garrison lost a dozen. In those days he used to say that he was seldom troubled with bits of silver, and had no need for a purse.

One morning a vessel from Newburyport, his dear native town, came into Baltimore harbour. She was named the *Francis*, and belonged to Mr. Ford, a Newburyport merchant, a man who was well known to Garrison. She lay there waiting for her cargo, and in a few days set her white sails and floated off to New Orleans. On board she carried eighty slaves. When Lloyd Garrison heard of it, he was so angry that a citizen of the free North should thus support the slave-trade of the South, that he published a fierce attack on the Newburyport merchant, who, in return, brought an action for libel against Garrison, and Garrison was summoned to trial in the Court-house at Baltimore.

There was great excitement and much rejoicing in the city when the trial was over, and it was known that the verdict was against "the madcap Garrison," and that he had been sentenced to pay a heavy fine. By that time the partnership with Benjamin Lundy had

been dissolved, for the partners had been
steadily losing money for some weeks. Lloyd
was too poor to pay the fine. Probably he
would not have paid it if he could do so. The
night after the trial was over he slept in
Baltimore prison. The first ray of sunlight
slanting in next morning through the high,
round window in his cell found him as happy
and peaceful as if he had wakened to a new
day in his safe home beside the sheltering
Green Mountains of Vermont. A long imprisonment lay before him. But as the days
passed by, the gaoler gave him increasing
liberty to wander at his will within the prison
walls. He made friends with his fellow-cap-
tives, and spent much time in helping and
advising them. Some of those men, when
they went back into the busy world, never
forgot words they had heard from Lloyd
Garrison in their quiet prison cells. Sometimes he came in contact with slave-traders,
who came there in search of runaway slaves.
For them he had a store of fierce and searching
words. In bygone times he had composed
poems as he wandered on Boston Common and
on the sunny Green Mountain slopes. Now,

no less contented in his gloomy prison cell,
happy thoughts came to him, and he left this
sonnet written on its walls,—

> " Prisoner, within these gloomy walls close pent,
>   Guiltless of horrid crime or venal wrong,
> Bear nobly up against thy punishment,
>   And in thy innocence be great and strong.
> Perchance thy fault was love to all mankind ;
>   Thou didst oppose some vile, oppressive law,
> Or strive all human fetters to unbind ;
>   Or wouldst not wear the implements of war.
> What then ?   Dost thou so soon repent the deed ?
>   A martyr's crown is richer than a king's !
> Think it an honour with thy Lord to bleed,
>   And glory 'midst intensest sufferings.
> Though beat, imprisoned, put to open shame,
> Time shall embalm and magnify thy name ! "

Thus the days passed away within his prison
walls.   Outside the prison, the story of Garrison's trial spread far and wide.   The general
verdict was that he had received his deserts.
Yet he had a few warm friends.   Of these, the
young poet Whittier was in great trouble on
his account, and Garrison's cheerful letters did
not console him.   He could not rest till he had
obtained his benefactor's release ; and day and
night the youth pondered over the means to be
taken for this end.   Now there was a Ken-

tucky statesman, Henry Clay by name, who
was slightly known to Whittier. He was a
wealthy man, and though he owned slaves, yet
he looked forward with hope to some distant
day when, with safety to their masters, and no
risk to the prosperity of the nation, they
might be set free. Mr. Clay could not help
admiring Garrison's courage and his faithful-
ness to what he thought was right; and when
John Greenleaf Whittier wrote to the Ken-
tucky senator, praying him to pay the fine and
set the guiltless prisoner free, he did not at
once refuse.

Meanwhile, Benjamin Lundy and Isaac
Knapp came to see their friend in prison, and
his old master, Mr. Allen, the printer, wrote
in the *Newburyport Herald* in his defence and
praise; and while Senator Clay still hesitated
and Whittier still made urgent appeals, a New
York merchant, named Arthur Tappan, came
forward and paid the fine.

So now Lloyd Garrison was again a free
man; but there was no longer any place for
him in Baltimore. Still, though he had not a
dollar in the world, he had strength and talent;
and life, with all its fresh chances, lay before

him. How should he use them all? Had he learned by this time to be silent when it was not safe to speak? Warning letters reached him, advising him to choose some safe, useful course in life, in which he might prosper. He was told that all his efforts against slavery would be useless, for what could one young man do when three millions were in chains, and a whole nation was against him.

But there was a voice within which spoke to Lloyd Garrison more clearly than did all those well-meant warnings, and this voice said: "Do what is right, and leave results to God." And Garrison listened and obeyed. He determined to go to the North again, and to set on foot an anti-slavery paper in the Free States. From there came the influence that supported slavery in the South, and he would labour night and day to waken the consciences of the Northerners, and rouse public opinion against that great sin that brought the North its wealth. A welcome gift of money paid all he owed; a free passage was given to him in a steamer to Rhode Island, and when landed there, he set forth on foot from city to city to deliver lectures against slavery. Sometimes

a night's shelter was given to him—most often
by Quakers; but few really warm welcomes
greeted him, except from the freed negroes.
Often he was forbidden to lecture, and the
doors of public rooms were closed to him. At
length he came to Boston, and there he sought
out statesmen, clergymen, and merchants, and
opened his heart to them; but one and all
made excuse. The old arguments were used—
cotton could only be obtained by slave-labour;
free men could not cultivate it. To free the
slaves at once would be unsafe for the masters,
and would bring the Union into danger. Texts
from the Bible were brought forward to prove
that slave-holding was no sin. One or two
people spoke of the hope of gradual emancipation, and of the possibility of establishing
distant colonies of freed negroes; but even for
such schemes, in their opinion, the time had
not yet come. Still, Garrison was not cast
down. Fresh cotton factories had sprung up
about the city since he had left it less than a
year before. There was no time to lose. He
must begin his work without supporters and
with no capital, and trust to God for help.

By-and-by the citizens of Boston were informed that a new paper, under the title of the *Liberator*, would be set on foot there by William Lloyd Garrison, and the motto of the paper ran thus,—

"Our country is the world; our countrymen are all mankind."

After he had made this announcement, Lloyd sought through Boston for some building in which he might give a lecture, and was resolved, if no room was granted to him, to speak on the open common to all who would come to listen. The only place he could obtain was the small hall where infidels in Boston held their meetings, and then he advertised a lecture in that room for Friday night, October 15th, and waited the result.

Surely these were dismal prospects for a youth who loved the companionship of his fellow-men, and had human longings for their sympathy. Might it not be that he was only risking safety and reputation for an idle dream? Was it not possible that those were wise warnings which declared his efforts against slavery could be of no avail? If such doubts sometimes crossed Lloyd Garrison's mind, they had no resting-place there, and the following sonnet which he wrote about this time tells another tale :—

> " How fall Fame's pillars at the touch of Time !
>   How fade like flowers the memories of the dead !
> How vast the grave that swallows up a clime !
>   How dim the light by ancient glory shed !
> One generation's clay enwraps the next,
>   And dead men are the aliment of earth ;
> Passing away is Nature's funeral text,
>   Uttered coeval with creation's birth.
> I mourn not, care not, if my humble namo
>   With my frail body perish in the tomb.
> It courts a heavenly, not an earthly, fame,
>   That through eternity shall brightly bloom.
> Write it within Thy Book of Life, O Lord,
> And in the last great day a golden crown award.'

CHAPTER IV.

THE "LIBERATOR."

IGHTY miles from Boston, in the village of Brooklyn, there lived a young minister, the Rev. S. J. May. His church was an ancient country meeting-house, and his parishioners were, for the most part, farmers. Some of his friends, who had known him in his college days, said that their old class-mate was wasting his powers in this quiet, uneventful life. He had a gentle nature and a winning voice and quick sympathies, and loved to live in peace with all men; but those who knew him best, knew that if ever a hard call of duty came, he would not shrink back from obeying it.

Early in the month of October, 1830, he paid

E

a visit to his father's house in Boston; and
while there, he learned that William Lloyd
Garrison, of whose imprisonment in Baltimore
he had heard, was going to give a lecture in
the Julian Hall. Mr. May resolved that he
would go to listen, and with him went his
cousin, Samuel Sewell, a rising Boston lawyer,
and another friend. Few well-known men
cared to be seen at such a place and for such
a purpose. The hall was only partly filled
when the lecturer began to speak, and we may
be sure that few signs of approval greeted him
as he gave his lecture. But at its close, the
young minister turned to his companions with
these words: "That is a providential man.
He is a prophet; he will shake our nation to
its centre, but he will shake slavery out of it.
Come, let us go and give him our hands."

So they went on to the platform, those three
young men, and held out their friendly hands
to the lonely hero, and his heart leaped for joy
as Samuel J. May said to him, in much-moved
tones: "I am sure you are called to a great
work, and I mean to help you." They did not
part till the city clocks struck midnight, and
till Garrison had convinced them that "*im-*

mediate emancipation was the right of every slave, and could not be withheld by his master for an hour without sin."

The following Sunday, the young minister from Brooklyn preached in one of the city churches. To the surprise and horror of the congregation, his theme was slavery, and he boldly upheld Garrison and his views. Next day, when the work-a-day world was astir, his old father was told by business men of the treasonable, fanatical language used by his son, and he was advised to arrest him, if possible, in his mad career. But in his quiet life, Samuel May had gained great courage to do right, and no arguments would now move him from his purpose. He went back to Brooklyn the disciple and follower of William Lloyd Garrison, and ready to work with him when the time came for action. This young minister was a Unitarian. Garrison was a Baptist, and had been brought up to believe that a man's salvation depended on his holding the orthodox belief. Perhaps he began now to think this a mistake. At all events, experience taught him in time that a religious life is shown in deeds, and not in creeds; and the

grasp of this good heretic's hand began a life-
long friendship that October night

But this new friend eighty miles away at
Brooklyn could not help Lloyd Garrison in
what he was about to do in Boston now, and
he must enter on the struggle without delay.
When a soldier marches out to battle, companions in arms are with him; trusted com-
manders urge him on; his blood is hot, and
he knows that the favour of his countrymen
is with him. For Garrison in *his* warfare it
was different. He was going to battle single-
handed, and, except for three or four distant
friends, all men were against him, and no voice,
except the whisper of his conscience, said, "Go
on."

The prospectus of the new paper was already
scattered over Boston. On the first morning
of the New Year 1831, the first number was
to be published. Only a little time was left
in which to find an office and a printing press,
and the "Mad-cap Garrison" had no subscribers and no capital.

In the third storey of a dingy building in
the city, beneath the eaves, he made his work-
shop and his home. The small windows were

bespattered with printer's ink; the wooden floor served him for a bed. A long deal table, a desk, some common chairs, and, in course of time, a second-hand printing-press, filled up the garret, and there he made this vow: " I will be harsh as truth, and as uncompromising as justice. I am in earnest. I will not equivocate; I will not excuse. I will not retreat a single inch, and I *will* be *heard.*"

> " In a small chamber, friendless and unseen,
>   Toiled o'er his type a poor, unlearned young man.
> The place was dark, unfurnitured and mean,
>   Yet there the freedom of a race began.
>
> Help came but slowly. Surely no man yet
>   Put lever to the heavy world with less.
> What need of help ? He knew how types were set,
>   He had a dauntless spirit, and a press."*

Isaac Knapp, the friend of Garrison's boyhood, knew also " how types were set," and he had not forgotten the old days when he and Lloyd used to talk together in Newburyport of the great things they hoped to do when they were men. And now, in this " day of small beginnings," he came to Boston, poor and unknown, to share his friend's toils and dangers,

* " The Day of Small Things," by James Russell Lowell.

and live and work with him in the obscure
garret where he had made his home. There
was a small baker's shop in the street below,
so they had not far to go for a loaf when they
needed food. They got a ream or two of
paper on credit for the first issue of the
Liberator, and a little money for other expenses came in from Mr. Sewell, the Boston
lawyer, and from another friend at a distance.

The New Year's morning dawned. The
Liberator lay in printed piles on the long deal
table, and any one who bought a copy that day,
after it was distributed through Boston, read
these words on the first page : " The publishers of the *Liberator* have formed their co-
partnership with a determination to print the
paper so long as they can subsist on bread
and water, or their hands find employment.
The friends of the cause may therefore take
courage : its enemies may surrender at dis-
cretion."

The little four-paged paper went out with
its message into the city streets. Busy men
whose trade it threatened, and prudent men
who held its schemes to be unwise and
premature, read it, and were sad or angry,

as the case might be. And Lloyd Garrison
and Isaac Knapp led lives of constant toil and
little sleep: and, though the bread shop stood
open in the narrow street below, they were
often hungry in those days. Each week a new
number came out, and Garrison was always as
" harsh as truth," and did not mince his words.
A few men in Boston, partially converted by
his words, sought him out in his garret, and
found the partners always hard at work and
hopeful—Garrison sitting at his desk writing
for the next week's issue. Sometimes he
might be seen with a favourite cat beside
him, rubbing her soft fur against him as he
wrote his articles; for he was tender at heart
still to both men and animals, and only savage
against their evil deeds.

Most welcome and dearest of all visitors was
Samuel J. May from Brooklyn. One day his
gentle nature recoiled from the biting words he
read in the *Liberator*, and he came to Boston
fearing that Garrison, in the heat and eagerness
of youth, was doing harm to the cause he had
at heart. On his arrival in the city, he went
to the *Liberator* office and found his friend,
as usual, in the cheerless garret. With the

winning voice and ways that were so dear to
Lloyd Garrison, he tempted him to come out
into the sunshine for an hour.   As they walked
together, using the freedom that their close
intimacy permitted, Mr. May turned to his
companion, and said, " Oh, my friend, do try to
moderate your indignation and keep more cool.
Why, you are all on fire."   Garrison stood still
and laid his hand on his friend's arm, while the
deep feeling within showed itself in face and
voice as he thus made reply: " Brother May,
I have need to be all on fire, for I have mountains of ice about me to melt."

And truly, like a firebrand, his messenger,
the *Liberator*, went out beyond Boston, through
the free Northern States and down into the
Southern Slave States.   Back came abuse and
threats and warnings that Garrison's life and
liberty were henceforth in danger; and at
last the Senate and House of Representatives
in Georgia offered to give a thousand dollars
to any person who would arrest the editor
of the *Liberator*, and bring him to trial and
prosecution.

Meanwhile, it was not only the slaves in the
distant cotton plantations of the South for

THE LIBERATOR.

VOL. I.]   WILLIAM LLOYD GARRISON AND ISAAC KNAPP, PUBLISHERS.   [NO. 17.

BOSTON, MASSACHUSETTS.]   OUR COUNTRY IS THE WORLD—OUR COUNTRYMEN ARE MANKIND.   [SATURDAY, APRIL 23, 1831.

THE LIBERATOR
IS PUBLISHED WEEKLY
AT NO. 11, MERCHANTS' HALL.

WM. LLOYD GARRISON, EDITOR.

TERMS.

THE LIBERATOR.

CHRISTIAN SECRETARY—COLONIZATION SOCIETY.

PRODUCTS OF SLAVERY.

whom Garrison was working. In Boston and
other cities of the North were little colonies of
Free Blacks who had bought their freedom or
escaped from slavery. These men were despised and ill-treated by the white men among
whom they lived. Few means of livelihood
were open to them. They were looked upon
as scarcely human. There were " negro pews "
set apart for them in churches and special
forms in schools, and it was a rare thing for a
coloured traveller to be admitted into a public
car or boat with white passengers. To earn
their daily bread was often a hard task, for no
coloured apprentice could find a place in any
shop where white men worked. Lloyd Garrison's love of justice and his pity were both
roused by the knowledge of the sad, crushed
lives of the Free Blacks ; and every week the
Liberator held appeals on their behalf. His
paper became their mouthpiece. He encouraged them to write for it, and urged
them, in its columns, to be sober and industrious, and to respect themselves, and learn
to be worthy of the good days that were yet
to come for them. " The time is not far
distant," he wrote, " when you and the

trampled slaves will all be free and enjoy the same rights in this country as other citizens. Prayer will forward the work faster than all the pens in the land. We can do nothing without it."

Few citizens of Boston were ever to be seen in the haunts of the Free Blacks. But Lloyd Garrison sought them out and made friends with them in their miserable homes. Deeds went with him hand in hand with words; and before long, a negro lad was to be seen working as apprentice with himself and Isaac Knapp at their printing press. For Garrison's heart ached for the hopeless-looking children growing up to share the despised condition of their fathers; and even in those days of his great poverty he would help one negro boy to rise.

In Boston was a famous Baptist preacher at this time—Dr. Lyman Beecher by name. Lloyd Garrison used to attend his church on Sundays. The vast building was crowded with worshippers, and echoed with their loud songs of praise; and Bible and tract societies, and missions to the poor, and good works of many kinds were set on foot by the preacher and his flock. But none of the Free Blacks were welcomed in that church as God's children, equal with the white men in His sight. Dr. Beecher disapproved of Garrison's zeal for the immediate abolition of slavery, and feared lest any excitement in the churches on such a subject might injure the great revival of religion, which he believed was daily gaining strength within them. " A strange religion ! " Garrison now began to say to himself ; and by degrees the belief grew up in his mind that Christianity and slavery could not exist together.

The busy days of 1831 were drawing to a close. The hours of daylight were few, and long, dark evenings had come. Still, threatening letters were sent to Garrison, and large rewards tempted needy men to kidnap the young editor on whose head a price was set. But Garrison knew no fear. He went about the city by day or night, when and where his duty led him, and laid plans for new efforts to be begun early in the coming year.

CHAPTER V.

THE FIRST ANTI-SLAVERY SOCIETY.

HERE was stormy weather in Boston when the new year, 1832, dawned. The snow lay thickly on the ground, and the east wind, with cutting blasts of hail, blew keenly. Few passengers were abroad, when, one night during the first week of the year, Lloyd Garrison and his partner made their way to a lonely part of the city, and ascended a steep, narrow street known as "Nigger Hill." No lamps ever broke the darkness of the winter's night in that part of Boston; but high up the hill-side a light was twinkling, and, thus guided, they reached at last the half-open door of a school-house, where the Free Blacks were accustomed to send their children to learn to read and write.

The two young men passed out of the storm
into the welcome shelter of the lighted room;
and there, in course of time, they were joined
by ten other white men. One of their number,
a Quaker hatter, named Arnold Buffum, was
chosen to take the chair, and they began the
business for the sake of which they had met
together. These twelve men might have been
a band of conspirators plotting against their
country, as they conferred together with closed
doors on that lonely, storm-swept hill. In
reality, they had met at Garrison's summons
to found the first anti-slavery society in
America; and one by one they followed him
to the table, and signed their names to the
new constitution. There were brave words on
that paper which should never be forgotten.
These men, on signing it, bound themselves to
rid their native land of the grievous wrong of
slavery, but to do so only by peaceful and law-
ful means, and to give no countenance to violence or insurrection. Truly, the young leader
of this little band had a mighty faith in the
power of moral influence; yet he was still
little more than a boy, living in a dreary garret, half starved on bread and water; but he

had found out betimes that all who work for the right have God upon their side, and he *knew* that his seemingly hopeless cause must win in the end.

When their work was done, and they all stood on the threshold of the school-house, looking out into the black, stormy night, Garrison turned to his companions and said : " We have met to-night in this obscure schoolroom. Our numbers are few and our influence limited ; but, mark my prediction, Faneuil Hall shall ere long echo with the principles we have set forth. We shall shake the nations by their mighty power." And with these hopeful words, the little company parted, and each man went his way to the perilous task he had undertaken.

Meanwhile the *Liberator* was carrying Garrison's appeals through the land, and rousing fresh workers. And here must be told the story of a brave woman who read Garrison's messenger, and answered nobly. In the pleasant country town of Canterbury, in Connecticut, there stood a large white house, overlooking the broad common. Prudence Crandall, a young Quakeress, had opened a school there, and every one in Canterbury knew

and respected Miss Crandall, and she and her
many scholars led happy, industrious lives. In
course of time, a girl, whose parents lived in
Canterbury, asked leave to enter Prudence
Crandall's school. She had been well trained
so far, but needed further help. No one in the
village could say a word against her, except
this—that her skin was not *quite* white. Now
Miss Crandall had read the *Liberator* for some
weeks past, and when it became known in
Canterbury that she had admitted the coloured
girl into her school, and she was warned that
such a step, if persisted in, would ruin her, she
grew bold, encouraged by Lloyd Garrison's
words, and replied: "My school may sink,
then, for I will not turn her out."   "Could
I not do more than this?" was the next
thought, as she read in the *Liberator* of the
multitudes of despised little ones among the
freed negroes for whom Garrison pleaded, and
whom so few men would help. And her next
act was to give up her flourishing school and
all her prospects in Canterbury, that she might
open her door to coloured girls only.

Prudence Crandall sought Garrison's help in
her new plan. He gladly sent her the scholars

she wanted; and very soon the well-known
school-house on the Canterbury common was
again filled with twenty happy, hard-working
girls.   But it was not long before troubles
began.   The people of Canterbury were indignant that Free Blacks should be treated in their
town as if they were white!   Public meetings
were held to protest against the school.   A new
law was passed prohibiting the establishment
of such an institution anywhere in the State of
Connecticut, in which the town of Canterbury
stood.   For a time Miss Crandall was im-
prisoned.   Mr. May and Mr. Arnold Buffum,
the white-haired president of the Anti-Slavery
Society, who came to her trial to defend her,
were refused a hearing.   One by one the shops
were closed against her; and had it not been
for the help of her father, who lived in Canterbury, she and her scholars might have
starved.   Her well was filled with rubbish;
rotten eggs and stones were thrown at her
house.   At one time it was set on fire.   No
doctor would visit the school, and the church
was closed against the inmates.   If they appeared in the streets, they were insulted and
hooted.   For two years Prudence Crandall

bravely persevered. At length a mob attacked the house at midnight, broke the windows with clubs and iron bars, and she was forced to close her school. But was this the end of all her self-sacrifice and courage? Had all her noble efforts been of no avail? No! Other men and women, who only needed such an example as she gave, were roused, by the tale of her endurance, to join the struggle and help Garrison and his little band. And so his influence spread, and here and there a new worker started up; and still Garrison said, " I will be heard. I will not retreat an inch ; I will be true as truth."

Certainly those were days in which there could be no standing still. Lloyd Garrison's efforts to educate the Free Blacks had wakened a new cry in the States. " Teach them if you must," some men were beginning to say ; " make them free and equal citizens, but not with the white men. Send them far away to some distant colony where white men have no place."

And with this watchword a new society had arisen, calling itself " The Colonization Society," and the design of its members was to send the

F

free negroes back to savage Africa, away from
the civilization which their labour had helped
to create.

Garrison saw how selfish and inhuman such
a scheme was. He knew, too, that it was but
a device to avert the dangers that threatened
the system of slavery—only a salve to the consciences of men who would not agree to the
immediate emancipation of the slaves. It was
the more needful, with this new enemy to face,
that Garrison and his band should work the
 harder. He was secretary of the lately formed
Anti-Slavery Society, and soon he was appointed agent to travel over the country and
give lectures and addresses. In addition to
this new employment, he wrote a pamphlet,
called "Thoughts on the Colonization Society," and sent it far and wide, in the footsteps
of the *Liberator*, to waken sympathy and speak
for justice for the Free Blacks. His twenty-
fifth birthday found him thus hard at work,
and he wrote in his journal that night: "Yes;
now I have struck deep into manhood. Well,
then, manhood shall be my most serviceable
stage, and, being so, the happiest of the whole."

Meanwhile, good news was coming to Garri-

son from across the sea in England. There,
great-hearted men, Wilberforce and the blind
Clarkson, Mr. Buxton, Joseph Sturge, and
many others, a noble army of workers, were
straining every power to set free the slaves in
the West Indian Islands, which were among
the English possessions. Like Garrison in
America, these men in England were demand-
ing *immediate* freedom for the slaves, and the
few voices which had first raised the cry were
gradually rousing the whole nation to see the
right, and declare that this justice must be
done. Among the English people were many
wealthy men ready to give help also to the
Anti-Slavery cause in America, and before long
a new task presented itself for Lloyd Garrison.
It was resolved that he should cross the ocean,
and tell his message in England, and also gain
funds here, if possible, to found a college for the
free coloured people in the States. Nor was
this the whole of his mission. An agent from
the Colonization Society was already in England, and Garrison, who had vowed to be harsh
as truth, must follow this agent and expose the
evils which lay at the basis of the scheme he
had gone to uphold.

The news of this proposed visit to England,
and Garrison's motives for making it, were soon
widely known, and from that time fresh perils
awaited him. His enemies were more anxious
than ever to seize him, and carry him away
prisoner to the Southern States. Each day
the danger increased. His friends trembled
for his safety as he went from city to city on
his lecturing tour. It was well known that
spies were watching for him, that writs on
false pretences were out against him, and that
agents from the South were seeking a chance
to serve them upon him, and carry him off by
cunning or by force. Still, he never shrank
from any duty. Passing quickly from place to
place, and so escaping capture, he gave addresses
and founded new branch Anti-Slavery Societies,
and gained funds for his mission to England.
At Philadelphia the freed negroes gathered
together to listen to him, and greeted him as
their deliverer, sobbing like children as they
pressed up to him to take his hands and tell
him how they loved and thanked him for his
noble work in their behalf. In course of time
he reached New York, whence he was to sail
for England. There was a delay of three days

in the departure of the ship, and during that
interval his friends knew well that it was unsafe for him to be seen in the city. On this
account, Mr. Arthur Tappan, the merchant to
whom in former days Garrison had owed his
release from prison at Baltimore, concealed
him in an upper room safely out of the reach of
the Southern agent, who was known to be on
the watch for him. On the first of May the
ship set sail, and in a few hours was out of
sight of land, bearing Lloyd Garrison towards
England. His name was well known there, and
brave, true men were ready to grasp his hand
in friendship. But whether lonely and hunted,
or honoured and in safety, this American hero
had a clear aim before him, and he cared not
where his way led, if only he could carry out
the work he had set himself to do.

A few words must tell of the sunny summer
days he spent in England. He found a kindly
welcome from the moment he landed in Liver-
pool, and at once was in the midst of the great
struggle which was agitating the whole country,
and growing stronger every day. He was
present at stormy debates in Parliament, and
heard how excuses were made and pleas were

brought forward in defence of slavery. He
joined in the eager watch for news from the
far-off West Indian Isles, where slaves and
planters in great excitement were awaiting the
result of the battle in the mother country
across the sea. And this self-taught, penniless
youth, made great and fearless by his devotion
to what was true and right, met with a hearing
wherever he went. Crowds in Exeter Hall,
in London, listened in deep silence to his
earnest words, while orators and statesmen,
famous through the world, gathered on the
platform and gave him their ready support.
He little knew how the story of his own brave
devotion to duty in the city of Baltimore and
the cheerless Boston garret had encouraged
those English workers to be firm and true, and
he in his turn went home the stronger for their
help and sympathy. Before he sailed from
England, the victory was won. The Bill which
was to set free 800,000 slaves had passed the
Commons. Before he landed in America, it
had received the Royal assent. In twelve
months' time the decree was to take effect, and
the West Indian slaves would all be free men.

When this news reached the United States,

the excitement it caused was intense. In the
South, the planters expected riots to break out
any moment among their slaves. In the North,
anger against Garrison waxed hotter, for with
the news came reports of his anti-slavery
speeches in England, and of his opposition to
the Colonization scheme. His return was
eagerly looked for. It was known that he was
to land in New York, and placards against him
were posted on the walls. On the day of his
arrival, threatening crowds collected in the
streets and in the neighbourhood of the harbour.
His first duty on landing was to attend an anti-
slavery meeting in the city. It was to no peaceful reunion of friends and followers that he
wended his way that night. Personally, he was
not well known in New York, and he could pass
safely through the angry mob in a way that
would have been impossible for him in Boston.
At the last moment, for the sake of safety, the
place of meeting was changed, and Garrison and
his fellow-workers assembled in a quiet, unpre-
tending chapel. But when their business was
over, as they were leaving by a door at the
back of the building, a furious crowd broke in
at the front, and the chapel echoed with shouts

for Garrison, and with yells and curses, while
the light shone on bowie knives and pistols,
and on the scowling faces of the invaders
disappointed of their prey. Such was Lloyd
Garrison's welcome home! But even while his
opponents thus sought his destruction, towards
them he had no bitterness of feeling. His only
wish was to deliver them from a deadly curse
and an awful sin.

CHAPTER VI.

"SHALL THE 'LIBERATOR' DIE?"

IN the quiet country at Haverhill, far away from the noise and strife of cities, the young poet, John Greenleaf Whittier, was living on the old farm among the meadows, while Lloyd Garrison was leading his busy life thus filled with anxiety and dangers. One evening in November, 1833, the early dusk was just hiding the hills and woods from sight, when a messenger from Boston entered the farmhouse with greetings from Garrison. It was a startling break in Whittier's peaceful life to hear that he was needed to join the workers against slavery, and that the brave man to whom he owed so much wanted his help at a great Convention which was about to meet in Philadelphia in a few days' time. Reports of angry mobs and city riots and ill-treatment of the Abolitionists had already reached Haverhill. Philadelphia lay on the borderland of slavery, and no one could deny that the proposed undertaking was a perilous one. But young Whittier was brave and true at heart. He had long been writing poems against slavery. Now he was ready, at Garrison's summons, for deeds. So his ready reply was, " I will go."

A great part of that night was spent in making plans for the care of the farm during his absence. Early the next morning, he took his place on the stage-coach for Boston, that he might join Garrison in that city, and travel in his company to Philadelphia. At New York and other places, fellow-travellers joined them, bound on the same errand as themselves; and they went on their way to Philadelphia. There were many subjects to discuss as they travelled. These men were all delegates from ten out of the twelve Free States in the Union, and Garrison had called them together to Philadelphia as their meeting-place, for the purpose of founding, for the first time, a *National* Anti-Slavery Society. By the time they reached their destination, they numbered

forty. Their first meeting was held in the
evening at the home of Evan Lewis, a simple,
earnest, hard-working man, neither wealthy nor
famous, of whom it was said that " he was
afraid of nothing but doing or being wrong."
The next day the first public meeting was to
be held, and no time must be lost in finding a
president. If possible, he must be a man well
known in the city.

So, forth into the night went Lloyd Garrison
and his friends, John Greenleaf Whittier and
Samuel J. May; and, calling at one great house
after another, they made their request; but in
vain. The chief citizens of Philadelphia made
excuses and gave cold receptions to the visitors
who asked their help. The scheme of immediate emancipation found no favour; the city was
in a state of excitement at the prospect of the
meetings. Indeed, the Mayor had declared that
the police could secure no protection to persons
assembling after nightfall with such a purpose
in view. For this reason the Convention was
to meet by daylight; yet no well-known citizen
would promise his countenance and support.

The night was far advanced when the three
friends came back to Evan Lewis' house and

told their tale of failure. What was to be done? Up rose a brave youth in the company, and, looking round on the perplexed faces about him, he said, "Well, if there is not timber among ourselves to make a president of, let us get along without one, or go home and stay there till we have grown up to be men." His advice was followed, and before they parted for the night, Beriah Green, an eloquent speaker, was out of their own ranks to preside at the meeting.

Early next morning rough men assembled in the streets of Philadelphia, and the approach of the delegates to the place of meeting was the signal for abuse and mockery. The hall was guarded by policemen, but no one was refused admission. Within gathered a little company of sixty-two men, mostly young in years, but strong in their opposition to slavery. Some were clad in plain, homespun garments fresh from their farms—some in Quaker garb. There were others who had left city offices, or schools and colleges, to attend the meetings. Among them were men whose homes were known to have been shelters for runaway slaves; women, such as Lucretia Mott who were ready to give

their lives to help on the anti-slavery cause;
strong youths who looked ready for a struggle
with the unruly mob then gathering outside the
doors; and gentler natures, like the peaceful,
sunny-faced Samuel May, who sat beside
William Lloyd Garrison, the leader of them
all.

All day the delegates held counsel; and as
dusk closed in upon the city, the meeting ended
to open again next day. It was resolved that
the first act of the members should then be to
sign a " declaration of principles." By this
declaration, the designs of the new society
would be made known, and also the work which
they pledged themselves to do. To Lloyd
Garrison was given the task of drawing up the
declaration : and while the other wearied delegates rested from their labours, he spent the
night in writing. Next morning his friends
sought him in his poor lodging under the roof
of a coloured man living in Philadelphia. They
found him still at work, his lamp burning just
as they had left it on the previous night, and
the daylight was making its way unnoticed
through the small attic window. Important
pledges, awaiting the signature of the delegates,

lay on the table before him—pledges to form
anti-slavery societies, as far as possible, in every
city in the land; to purify the churches from
any share in the guilt of slavery; to send forth
lecturers to keep the subject before the public,
and to spare no exertions to bring the whole
nation to speedy repentance of the great
national sin.

Such promises, with others of like nature,
were laid before the assembly. A long discussion followed. It would be no easy task to keep
these pledges: the effort to do so would involve
great labour—possibly also risk to liberty and
life. What wonder if at first some of the
listeners shrank back from signing the paper
which their fearless leader had drawn up? For
the last time the declaration was read aloud by
Samuel J. May. As he read, his voice was
broken by emotion, so deeply did he feel the
meaning of the words. A solemn silence fell
upon the little company. It was broken at
length by the sound of footsteps, as one person
after another, without speaking, advanced to
the platform and signed. Thus was formed
the American Anti-Slavery Society: and with
these new pledges, the members parted from

each other, and went forth their separate ways into the world.

Travellers on mountain-heights far above human dwellings find the sources of mighty rivers in streamlets that trickle from beneath the everlasting snows. From little seeds taking root and germinating in fertile soil have arisen the vast forests that clothe the surface of the earth. In like manner, some of the grandest reformations of the world are due to the thoughts and work of a few faithful souls. Only three years had passed since Garrison and his brave companions had met in the little school-house on the lonely, windswept hill, to found the first anti-slavery society in Boston. Now the American Anti-Slavery Society with its delegates from ten States, had given to the movement a *national* basis. Garrison could witness the progress of his work and an increasing number of helpers; but he could also see fresh dangers threatening. For as the anti-slavery party worked harder and became more widely known, so did the opposition to it increase. Riots broke out in cities where meetings were held, the houses of the Abolitionists were attacked. and slavery was defended more strongly than ever by both pulpit and press.

For many months past, Garrison's thoughts, in the midst of his excitement and hard work, had turned to a peaceful dwelling where he had sometimes been received as an honoured guest. The memory of its happy family circle shone like a bright light over the pathway of this lonely, homeless man. The house stood in a large garden among the hills near Brooklyn, and there lived Mr. George Benson, once a busy merchant in the town of Providence. Now he had given up the cares of business, and devoted his time and strength to help the cause of the oppressed slaves. In old days, Mr. Lundy had stayed there as he wandered over the country with his pack on his back to sell his anti-slavery papers : and more recently, Prudence Crandall and her pupils had found firm friends in Mr. Benson and his family.

In this home, in the year 1834, William Lloyd Garrison found the loving woman who became a faithful helpmate to him, in Helen Benson, the youngest daughter of the family. She was so sunny in her temper, and so large-hearted and unselfish, that her friends used to call her

" Peace and Plenty." Honouring Garrison as she did, for his noble, self-denying life, when she found that he loved her, Helen Benson could see no better lot for herself than to share his cares. So in the autumn of that year their simple wedding took place, and they made a new home in a cottage among the woods at Roxbury, three miles from the heart of Boston, where the *Liberator* office stood. They were very poor; but poverty and happiness may go hand in hand. Isaac Knapp lived with them and helped to pay the rent of their tiny dwelling, to which they gave the name of " Freedom's Cottage."

This newly found joy never interfered with Garrison's work. The leading articles in the *Liberator* neither failed not flagged, and business often kept him so late at the printing office that he walked home at midnight along the lonely country road. On such occasions, unknown to him, his friends among the freed negroes used to make a point of following him at a distance, lest he should be waylaid and murdered; and they only turned back to the city when the light from the cottage shone out upon the night as the door opened to admit

G

him. Happily his young wife, waiting for him at home, knew nothing of the faithful body-guard, nor of the need for such defence.

During the summer of 1834, tidings, for which both England and America had been anxiously watching, came from the West Indian Islands. They told how the slaves on the plantations there had at last received their promised liberty. The great day of emancipation had come and gone : the slaves had assembled in their island chapels when the first of August arrived, to await there for the midnight hour that was to set them free. Amid prayers and hymns and cries of joy, they greeted their new life. Neither rioting nor bloodshed took place; and after a short holiday, peacefully spent, the negroes gathered again upon the old plantations to work as free men for fair wages. Was it any wonder that such tidings gave Garrison fresh spirit for his work? and yet sometimes even to him the task he had undertaken seemed well-nigh hopeless. The *Liberator*, after all his efforts, did not pay expenses, and there were increasing arrears of debt which must be met.

"Shall the *Liberator* die?" was the question

with which he again and again appealed in its
pages to his subscribers. The outlook was
gloomy. His young wife told him merrily that
it suited her to live on bread and water : and
truly it seemed as if his work for humanity
threatened to bring starvation on his own home.
Still, though to this was added the knowledge
that his life was often in danger, Garrison felt
the peace of mind which comes from duty
faithfully done, and he could say of his greatest
trials and perplexities, " They cannot reach up
to the level of my home mood."

Moreover—and this was a great relief—a
new helper was on his way to Garrison from
England. His arrival might be expected any
day. " He is coming among us as an angel of
mercy. His name is as sweet as the tones of a
flute to my ear." Thus Garrison wrote in the
Liberator of the young Englishman, who was
no other than George Thompson, a great orator,
whose energies had been turned against slavery
in the West Indies for years past. The victory
won in England twelve months before had been
in great measure due to his labours. He was a
young man about Garrison's own age ; and
through the anti-slavery struggle in his own

land, he had served as lecturing agent for the
London Anti-Slavery Society, drawing crowds
wherever he went, to listen to his wonderful
eloquence.

It will be remembered that while Garrison
was in England, seeking help for his uphill
conflict in America, the West Indian Emancipation Bill passed the House of Lords. Then
George Thompson's work was done; and when
Garrison was asked by the English leaders, "In
what way can we best help *your* cause?" he at
once replied, "By giving us George Thompson."
The young English orator had promised to
follow Garrison to the United States to begin
a new anti-slavery lecturing tour there : and it
mattered not to him that Garrison said he could
offer him "no reward of any kind, except that
which comes from doing well." Still, in his
own heart, Garrison had fondly hoped that
George Thompson had only to speak to con-
vince all hearers, and that with his help, slavery
must soon end in America.

So now, when each ship that entered New
York harbour might bring this English helper
among her passengers, Garrison was eagerly on
the watch for news of his arrival. But he had

discovered by this time that no easy path of
victory awaited George Thompson. He was
already denounced by press and pulpit, and held
as an enemy to American institutions, as one
who, with the help of British gold, was bent
on destroying the union of the Northern and
Southern States. So strongly was public
opinion known to be against him, that an honest
pilot, who wished every man to have fair play,
spoke these words of warning to the chaplain of
a ship at that time about to enter New York
harbour : " If you have George Thompson on
board, hide him for the sake of his life." By
the time the newly landed English orator
met Garrison in Boston, he had strange ex-
periences to relate of the rough greeting he had
already met with in America. Happily there
was another story to tell also of glad welcomes
sent to him from anti-slavery societies scattered
over the States, and a hopeful little company
gathered round the log fire in Garrison's cottage
to talk over future plans, while the bleak night
winds blew fiercely through the woods at Roxbury.

CHAPTER VII.

THE BOSTON MOB.

HE year 1835 was known in America as the "great mob year." Garrison's story leads us now into scenes of violence and hair-breadth escapes—in days when every man who dared to uphold the cause of the slaves carried his life in his hand. In 1831, when the unknown young printer had just raised his voice against slavery in Boston, no one but he ventured to *whisper* the suggestion of immediate freedom for the slave, and even the plan of gradual emancipation was scarcely breathed. But the little torch he so bravely carried in that darkness had lighted a mighty fire which no man could put out. So, as the months went by, the excitement waxed fiercer and fiercer, and at length a reign of terror was reached. In 1835,

the old days of the French Revolution were
brought to mind in the cities of the United
States. No man could trust his neighbour;
private assassins lurked at the corners of the
streets, and there was no security of life or
property for a suspected Abolitionist. The
fierce cry rose against Garrison and his band
of workers,—" You shall not succeed in your
efforts; we mean to put you down by fair
means if we can—by foul means if we must,"
and the mere discussion of the subject of slavery
was looked upon as treason against the government and union of the States. *Still*, Garrison
hoped to win the right by peaceful means and
moral influence alone.

Freedom's Cottage, in the woods at Roxbury,
stood empty towards the end of 1835; for
Garrison and his brave young wife went to live
in Boston, so as to be in the midst of the
coming struggle. John Greenleaf Whittier, too,
had given up his poet's paradise and all the
delights of his home at Haverhill. Not content
with writing " Songs of Freedom," which gave
magical courage to the brave heroes who looked
upon him as their poet and prophet in that
stormy time, he, too, became a worker; and, as

secretary of the National Anti-Slavery Society,
and editor of a paper at Philadelphia, he entered
on a business career which was opposed to all
his tastes and wishes. Thus, of his own free
will the poet put aside the life which was so
dear to him, and followed Garrison's leading,
while startling events befel him in quick succession. At one time his office was burned
over his head; at another he rode for his life
through the city streets, 'mid a storm of stones
and bullets; more than once he was mobbed
with George Thompson. No wonder if sometimes his thoughts turned with longing to the
quiet meadows and still windings of the river
at Haverhill. No wonder that, when one day
musing of his forsaken paradise, he wrote,—

> " Oh! not of choice, for themes of public wrong,
> I leave the green and pleasant paths of song."

Meanwhile George Thompson had been lecturing for nearly twelve months in the States.
Wherever he went, he left behind him undying
memories of wonderful eloquence; and new
friends rose up at his words, to help the anti-
slavery cause. But he roused enemies also.
The notice of a lecture to be given by him in

any city became the signal for a mob. He
went to and from the place of meeting at the
risk of his life. Brickbats and stones saluted
him, and cries of "Lynch him" were the greetings of the rioters. When his name was
spoken in public, it was as if a fire-brand had
been thrown into the midst of the crowd. And
it came to pass, at last, that even Garrison
sadly acknowledged that the English orator
must take his leave. After this, it became a
question how to save his life until such time as
he could safely embark for England. Unknown
to all, except a few faithful friends, he was
secreted for some weeks in Boston, waiting the
departure of a small English brig bound for
St. John's. From that port he could set sail
across the ocean.

Work connected with the *Liberator* filled
Garrison's days, and sometimes his nights.
Anti-slavery publications were sent down by
thousands into the Southern States, and caused
a panic there. The mails were seized, money
rewards for the heads of Garrison and Thompson were offered from all parts of the South.
They were hung in effigy before the door of
Garrison's house in Boston. It became more

and more difficult to hire a hall in any city for
the purpose of an anti-slavery meeting. Every
attempt to raise the condition of the freed
negroes in the North was crushed as it arose.
A school opened for coloured people roused the
opposition of a whole State, and the building
was speedily a heap of ruins. Even peaceful
Haverhill was the scene of a riot, and the
gentle Samuel May, when lecturing there, was
mobbed by a wrathful crowd.

Such news reached Garrison day by day; yet
still his faith was firm that right must win in
the end, and still he said, as he had said in
former days, "I will not retreat an inch. I
will not equivocate. I will be heard." But
let no one think that it cost him little pain to
stand so much alone, and to know the hatred
he brought on himself by his work and words.
It was true that he wore a brave face as he
met the rioters in the streets, and that his
words were fearless and stern in the *Liberator;*
but a kind and unexpected greeting from a
stranger touched him so deeply in his loneliness as to break the strong man down; and
hardest of all to him was the need, which
sometimes came, of acting in opposition to

his friends in what he felt it right to do and
say.

The month of October in that "great mob
year" drew near, and the thoughts of all anti-
slavery workers centred in Boston; for on
the 21st of October, a meeting of the Women's
Anti-Slavery Society was to be held in the Anti-
Slavery Hall, adjoining the *Liberator* office in
that city, and there was no hope that the day
would be allowed to pass without disturbance.
It was to be no secret meeting with closed
doors. Those Boston women, few in number,
dared to be true to the right in face of public
scorn, and fearless of the danger they incurred.
Garrison calmly helped in the preparations,
placarded the meeting over the city walls, and
arranged to be present and give an address.

More than fifty years have passed since that
day, and still the need of women's influence
against wrong is as great now as it was then.
So it is well that the story of these brave
Boston women, who left their sheltered homes
that October morning to face an angry mob,
should not be forgotten. A false rumour had
been spread abroad that George Thompson
would attend the meeting; and on the morning

of the day the following notice appeared upon
the walls : " *Thompson the Abolitionist.* That
infamous foreign scoundrel will attend the
meeting at the *Liberator* office this afternoon.
The present is a fair opportunity for the friends
of the Union to snake Thompson out. It will
be a contest between the Abolitionists and the
friends of the Union. A price of one hundred
dollars has been raised to reward the individual
who shall first lay violent hands on Thompson,
so that he may be brought to the tar-kettle before dark. Friends of the Union, be vigilant ! "

The Anti-Slavery Hall was up some flights
of stairs, and was divided from the *Liberator*
office by a wooden partition. In this room,
before three o'clock in the afternoon, the members of the society, both white and coloured
women, gathered together; and in the streets
below, a surging crowd collected to watch for
the foreign scoundrel Thompson, and for " the
mad-cap Garrison." Garrison, however, was
already in the hall; and as the rioters pushed
up the narrow staircase, the foremost of them
mounted on the shoulders of their strong companions to peer in at the ladies seated quietly
in the room, a cry was raised, " That's Garri-

son," and was answered by shouts of rage from below. For a few moments afterwards there was an astonished silence on the part of the intruders as Garrison advanced to them and spoke in defence of the ladies, and the privacy of their meeting. Then again the storm broke forth, and shrieks, and howls, and hisses rose up from the crowds as they pressed more closely up the narrow street. "Out with the scoundrel! Here's Garrison!" was the continual cry. It was evident that his presence only excited rage, and the lady president besought him to withdraw to the *Liberator* office, behind the wooden partition. Seated there, Garrison could hear the solemn voice of the president, in her opening prayer, thank God that while there were so many to molest, none could make them afraid. And once more burst forth fresh threats and curses and deafening noise when the secretary tried in vain to read the Annual Report. Still the little band of women remained, each one in her place, though missiles were thrown and the secretary was struck. A shout arose of "The Mayor is coming!" and straightway forcing their way up the staircase came a strong force of constables, with the Mayor at their head, and with him some of Garrison's friends.

"Go home, ladies!" cried the Mayor. "Do you wish to see a scene of bloodshed? If not, go home! I can protect you now; in a little while this will be impossible." So two and two they descended the stairs, and the Boston women of gentle birth each walked beside a coloured woman, to protect her from the mob that waited in the streets below. There the crowd, with a roar of rage and contempt, parted to let them pass; and they saw among the scowling faces those of "gentlemen of standing and position," whom in quieter days they had known as their friends.

Meanwhile, Mrs. Garrison had been prevented from reaching the meeting-place by the mob. She waited at home for her husband's return; but hour after hour passed, and he did not come. At last, rumours reached her of the tumult in the city. She was young, and tenderly attached to him, and all her maiden life had been passed in the sunshine of a safe and happy home. But never for a moment did she wish to turn him away from any danger into which his duty led him. That night, when a friend came to tell her what had befallen him, she made answer, "I believe my husband will be true to his principles."

Surely William Garrison had found a help-mate in his wife.

Round the *Liberator* office, the swaying, swelling crowds cried out for Garrison. "We must have Garrison! Out with him! Lynch him!" And within sat their victim, with calm and peaceful face, with no sign of fear; nor had he any anxious thought, save on his wife's account.

Not so his friends, who had forced their way up the staircase through the tightly packed rioters, and now did not know how to save him from their fury.

"Throw us out Garrison! Lynch him!" yelled the mob in the street below, and the ruffians on the stairs battered on the wooden door that the Mayor had locked behind him. "Let us fight a way for Garrison!" cried some one, and his friends prepared to lead the way and open a path for him with blows. Then outspoke this hero, true to his vow of using peaceful means and moral influence alone,—

"You do not know what spirit you are of. Would you like to become like those violent, bloodthirsty men who are seeking for my life? Shall we give blow for blow? God forbid! I will die sooner than raise my hand against any man, even in self-defence, and let none of my friends resort to violence for my protection. If my life be taken, the cause of emancipation will not suffer. God reigns. His throne is unmoved by the storm. His truth will at length be victorious."

While Garrison was speaking, the Mayor held a hurried consultation with the constables. The crowd would not disperse, it was agreed, while Garrison was in the building. He must leave it by a back window. But this new design was discovered, and the mob, surging and yelling, tore round to the back in time to seize Garrison as he lighted from the roof of a shed on to the ground. In an instant, with torn clothes, and bareheaded, he was dragged along the streets by means of a rope thrown round his body, 'mid cries of "They've got him! they've got him!" Could it be, as people said, that he had a smile upon his face? The crowd followed, hooting. As the Mayor turned into

Portion of Plan of Boston, enlarged from Smith's map,
1835, showing: **A**, Anti-Slavery Offices, Washington Street;
and **B**, City Hall (Old State House).

[Face p. 96.

the street, he was met by the shout, "They're going to hang him! For God's sake, save him!"

On by a short cut to the city hall sped Mayor and constables. Garrison and his captors, dragging him by the rope, must pass the building. The constables seized the right moment, and pulled him through the doorway, while a yell of disappointed rage went up from the maddened mob. But there was no resting-place for Garrison in the city hall. The Mayor, though the Boston mob held him somewhat in awe for the sake of his office, was not a man who could be firm as a rock when justice and fair play were at stake. He must get rid of this disturber Garrison at all costs, and concluded that the safest place to lodge him in for the night was the city jail. Accordingly, two lines of constables were formed, and Garrison was passed out between them, and hurried into a coach. The driver lashed his horses, and hit with his whip the heads and hands of the men who sprang forward to seize the reins and cling to the carriage wheels. The horses plunged and reared, and the living mass gave way before the rocking coach, then formed

again, and tore up the streets in pursuit. When
dusk settled down upon the city, Garrison was,
for the second time in his life, a prisoner.
Whittier and Isaac Knapp visited him, and
talked with him through the grated window of
his cell, and carried his cheering message to
his wife.

So ended the Boston mob; and peaceful
sleep visited this man, who would not strike a
blow in self-defence, yet did not fear " to be in
the right with two or three," though the multitude raged against him.

Next morning he was set at liberty. But
the Boston authorities begged him for the
peace of the city to absent himself for a time;
and, avoiding all public conveyances, which
were being searched in the hope of capturing
him, Garrison left Boston, and followed his
wife into the country.

CHAPTER VIII.

DISCORDS IN THE CAMP.

LL really great heroes have tender, gentle hearts. This American hero was no exception to the rule. Although hard pressed by poverty, and hunted by fierce enemies, the kindly greetings of friends had power to call forth his responso in a moment, and the voices of little children, or the sound of music, could waken sunshine within him in the darkest hour. His wife knew how true the saying was that no trials nor anxieties could reach up to his home mood. Early in 1836 the first boy came to gladden their home. He was named George Thompson. There could be no more tender father than Garrison, whose rebukes were so unsparing and severe against the sin of slavery. At night, he often spent long hours in hushing

the little restless baby to sleep, that the mother
might have undisturbed repose. Yet his own
health broke down after the treatment he received from the Boston mob. Attacks of fever
visited him, and for a year or so he was un-
able to undertake any active work for the
anti-slavery cause. Still, wherever he was,
his influence never ceased to make itself widely
felt. It is a true saying that "the blood of
the martyrs is the seed of the Church." As in
the early days of Christianity the persecution
of the Roman emperors only added new members to the Christian flock, so in the "martyr
age of America," fresh workers sprang up to
follow Garrison's banner.

Meanwhile, wonders had been wrought in
Philadelphia, where, in 1833, Whittier had gone
at Garrison's call, to help to found the American Anti-Slavery Society. A great building
had been afterwards erected there by the
friends of freedom, and on May 17th, 1838,
it was to be opened for public use, and dedi-
cated to the free discussion of questions of
liberty, education, and temperance. On the
appointed day, anti-slavery workers, who had
gathered together at Philadelphia from various

parts of the States, turned their steps in the bright spring sunshine to Pennsylvania Hall. For three days meetings were held there. On the evening of the third day it was noised abroad through the city that William Lloyd Garrison, among other speakers, would address the assembly; and at an early hour the hall was densely filled. Three thousand persons were present. The floor of the hall was covered with women. The side aisles and wide galleries were closely packed with men. All *seemed* to betoken good order; but in reality the streets outside were quickly filling with excited people, for whom no standing room could be found in the hall. William Lloyd Garrison rose to speak, and his subject was the *immediate* emancipation of the slaves. He was very eloquent, and spoke strongly against half measures and delay in doing right. The close of his speech was the signal for a terrible uproar. The mob outside the building began to dash in the windows with stones, and to yell and rage outside the doors.

At this juncture up rose Mrs. Chapman, a Boston woman, well known for her interest in anti-slavery work, to address for the first time a large assembly; and after her, one brave woman after another, believing that all gentle influences were needed that memorable day, spoke in Pennsylvania Hall—among them Mrs. Weld (Angelina Grimke), Lucretia Mott, Esther Moore, and Abby Kelley, still almost a girl, from the country town of Lynn. It was not strange that, from that time, Garrison asked more earnestly than ever for the help of women in his work, or that he tried to teach that no one was unwomanly who used for right and gentle ends the power and influence God gave her.

That day life and property in Philadelphia were spared, but only for a few hours. Next night, Pennsylvania Hall was set on fire by the mob, and the light of the burning building was seen for miles round—a witness to the result of the ungoverned passions of men, while the homes and churches, and even the persons of the coloured people in the city, suffered injury at the hands of the rioters.

From city to city in the North this brutal spirit which tried to put down free speech by force had spread, till the reign of terror reached its height. For an Abolitionist to venture into

the Southern States was to risk his life; and
it was an offence against public opinion to oppose slavery in almost any society, for slavery
was held to be the "corner-stone of the Re-
public," and men were traitors to the State, it
was said, who would thus endanger the Union.
But even the most resolute slave-owner began
to see that no mob violence could put an end
to the anti-slavery agitation, and a new atti-
tude must be assumed. From the slave-holders
and their Northern friends came very frequent
demands for laws to be passed against the
Abolitionists, that these disturbers of the peace
and treason-mongers should be punished with
death.

Now in Boston at this time, Dr. Channing
was one of the best known preachers. No one
in the city was more respected and admired
than he. Hitherto he had held aloof from the
great struggle that was going on, and spoke
gravely against Garrison's bitter language in
the *Liberator*, and against the outbreaks of
passion in the cities of the Northern States,
that were roused by the action of the Abolitionists. For he was a lover of peace, and looked
on quarrels among men who should live as

brethren, as terrible evils. Garrison and his friend, Mr. May, had often spoken together about the great influence Dr. Channing might have in helping on their work. Garrison had written to him in vain to this effect. Perhaps there was no man for whom the Brooklyn minister had greater reverence. He had re-collections of Dr. Channing's great influence over his own boyhood; and in youth and man-hood, the great preacher had been to him both a prophet and a saint. So it was a grief to him that such a leader of men as Dr. Chan-ning should remain silent about, and apart from, the great struggle to which by that time he had consecrated his own life. Now Samuel May felt such reverence for this wise man who had been the guide of his youth, that it would have been an easier task for him to oppose a mob of rough and ignorant men than to seek out Dr. Channing to tell him that he was neg-lecting a duty. But since he had come under Garrison's influence, the gentle-hearted, peace-loving man had never any dread of standing alone for a principle, nor did he now hesitate to do this task which he felt conscience called him to undertake. So he travelled to Boston, was admitted to Dr. Channing's study, and there their talk turned on the anti-slavery struggle, and on the violent measures which Dr. Channing so much deplored. As the younger man heard the thrilling tones of the voice that had such power over men, he felt a great longing to gain his influence in the cause, and thus he spoke: "God has called to the work many mighty men, and they have not answered. We have come from the hedges and ditches, highways and byways, and are here to do the work. Look to it, sir, for the work in the Master's vineyard will surely be done. Is it not time, sir, that you spoke?"

The greatest men are the most willing to be learners, and are never afraid to acknowledge their mistakes. Dr. Channing kept silence for a little while, and then he made this answer to the eager young man, whom he had known as a little child: "Brother May, I feel the justice of your reproof. I *have* kept silence too long." Not long afterwards the Northern and Southern States of America were roused to great excitement. A powerful book against slavery issued from the press. It was by Dr. Channing. It was widely read, and there was no

longer any doubt on which side the popular
preacher stood.

And now comes the story of the great meeting in Faneuil Hall—the large building in
Boston that has won the name of "the Cradle
of Liberty," where men of Boston gathered
together at Dr. Channing's appeal to defend
freedom of the press. Terrible news had come
from the town of Alton, in Illinois, where the
editor of a newspaper—Elijah P. Lovejoy, had
bravely written in his columns in defence of
a down-trodden, brutally treated slave, and had
pledged himself to defend the cause of human
rights, and to die, if need be, in their defence.
Three times his printing-press had been destroyed by a mob in Alton. A fourth press
had arrived upon the scene, and been placed in
the office ready for the next day's work. That
night, Mr. Lovejoy and some of his friends
kept watch in the printing-office to insure the
safety of the press. Long before dawn they
heard the tramp of feet break on the silence.
Men were gathering outside, and shortly the
cry of "Turn them out: fire the building,"
greeted the watchers' ears. A short struggle
followed. The brave editor was shot through

the heart, and the ruffians, who wished to
prevent liberty of the press in Alton, forced
their way into the building, destroyed all
before them, broke up the new printing-press,
and threw the pieces into the river Mississippi
which flowed below.

When this news came to Boston, it was
freely discussed. Pulpits and newspapers defended the rioters, or made excuses for their
deed. Was not Lovejoy an Abolitionist? it was
asked. At all hazards must not such men be
silenced? Dr. Channing loved peace, but he
also loved free speech, and he was deeply
moved by this murder of Mr. Lovejoy, and by
this triumph of brute force over right. Truly,
the warning he had received was a just one.
It was time that he spoke; for men of influence must lend their voices to defend
freedom of thought and speech. So that night,
when the great meeting was held, the walls of
Faneuil Hall echoed with the cheers of Boston
citizens, whose better selves were quickened by
the burning, indignant words of Dr. Channing;
and Wendell Phillips, a young rising lawyer,
whom Garrison had called to the work a few
weeks before, risked reputation and success in

life, and followed with so noble a speech that
it never left the memories of those who heard
it.   There was a contrast! on the one hand,
the tyranny of brute force on the part of the
lawless mob at Alton; on the other hand, the
influence of the moral enthusiasm of men in
Faneuil Hall, who *knew* the right must win in
the end.   The little stone which the boy Garrison had set rolling years before had gathered
as it rolled, and his prophecy that Faneuil Hall
should echo with the principles set forth by a
handful of men in the lonely school-house on
" Nigger Hill " was realized.   The news of this
great public meeting, when it reached him,
while he was still suffering from the treatment
of the Boston mob, seemed to him like a song
of triumph.

During the years in which Garrison's influence had been slowly making way in the
North, two sisters, named Sarah and Angelina
Grimke, had passed their happy girlhood in the
Southern States at Charleston, in South Carolina.   Their father was a well-known judge,
and when he died, they lived together in their
pleasant home in the midst of a large circle of
old friends.   "An easy, prosperous life lies

before them," it was said; but such speakers
little knew that beneath all this apparent comfort the sisters' hearts were aching at the sight
of the sorrows and degradations of the women
who were in slavery around them. They read
Garrison's *Liberator* and the other anti-slavery
papers which made their forbidden way into
the Southern States: and at last a strong feeling of duty led them to give up home and
friends and property in that land polluted by
slavery, and to go northwards to Philadelphia,
self-exiled among strangers, to try what they
could do in helping on the struggle that was
being waged there against this terrible wrong.

After a while, Angelina wrote and published
a short appeal to women of the South against
slavery. It was only a little pamphlet, but
its words came straight from her heart. She
was asked to go to New York to speak to
women on the subject in a private house in the
city. She went, and her earnestness made her
eloquent. Time after time, wives and mothers
and sisters listened to her and carried home
the story of her words. At length, large
assemblies of both men and women gathered
in public halls to listen to this woman, who,

from her own experience, could tell so truly of
the cruelty and wickedness of the slavery by
which the Northern merchants made their
wealth.

When Mrs. Chapman, for conscience' sake,
rose up for the first time to address the great
Convention in Pennsylvania Hall, while the mob
stormed and raged outside, it was to do no
pleasant, easy work. Lucretia Mott, and
Esther Moore, and Abby Kelley, and Prudence
Crandall, and a host of other women, whose
hearts were bleeding with pity for the slaves,
followed the hard call of duty when they took
up the anti-slavery work. Was it surprising
that when Garrison found these noble, self-
sacrificing women among his best helpers, he
demanded that they should be enrolled as
members of the anti-slavery societies in which
they worked, and allowed to vote and speak
when anti-slavery meetings were held ? He
was eager to join hands with *all* good workers.
In his opinion, friends of freedom should meet
on common ground, without regard to creed,
or politics, or sex.

After a struggle the American Anti-Slavery
Association fell in with his views and elected

women as members. But serious results followed this new step. Old companions and fellow-workers of Garrison could not sympathize with this and other plans that he felt it was right to set on foot. Discords arose. A branch society was formed, and the strength of the anti-slavery party was weakened by the division. Mr. Arthur Tappan was the leader of this new party. Garrison was deeply pained. He owed very much to the good New York merchant who years before had freed him from the Baltimore prison, and had often shown him sympathy and given him help in later times. He would have gladly given way to Mr. Tappan's wishes if it had been in his power to do so. But principle was at stake : he must be true to the right, and therefore he sadly parted from his friend. Other partings as painful followed this one. Garrison was a man of peace, and hoped to rid the land of slavery by peaceful means alone. Old friends, burning with zeal, found fault with his measures, and said that influence alone could never win the day. They, too, joined the new association. So, just when the outlook seemed to be brightening, when 2000 anti-slavery societies were in the field, and Garrison had gathered a noble army together, the new organization was formed, and the division changed the strength into weakness.

And now harder trials fell upon this American hero than those which had come from the ill-usage of mobs or the threats of Southern assassins; for his fellow-country-men began to give him the hard names of athiest and unbeliever, of Sabbath-breaker, and enemy to the Christian religion. " He is a heretic," they cried; " his views are unsound. If we could get rid of Garrison and his friends, many of the clergy and laymen of influence would help in the struggle. There is no room for such as he on the anti-slavery platform."

Such were the hard words spoken at this time of the man to whom the noble work so far done was due. They were spoken by men who could not see how deeply religious he really was, or how his deeds and words sprang from true love to God and man. He was called a Sabbath-breaker because he did not scruple on Sundays, if he had the chance, to speak or write in defence of the down-trodden slaves. "A man's religion," so he said, "must be shown by acts of mercy to his fellow-men."

Garrison wished to make all days holy days by filling them all with good deeds. He was called an atheist and an unbeliever because he turned away from all connection with the churches and clergy that upheld slavery. " Christianity can have no complicity with slave-holders," he cried. So long as men high in position in the churches kept slaves and the clergy supported the slave system from their pulpits, so long he believed they would all be false to Christ's religion of love, and their churches could be no true branches of the Church of God. His views were said to be unsound because, when men brought forward texts from the Old Testament to sanction slavery, he answered that though the Bible was the best of all books, it must be judged like other human compositions; for it told the story of the gradual education of the human race, and texts which ran counter to the commands of conscience to-day sprang from the mistaken ideas of men in their early gropings after right.

The new organization was called the National Anti-Slavery Society. Its formation was the cause of much rejoicing to the supporters of slavery. " See ! " they said, " by this split in

I

their ranks our enemies are putting *themselves* down." Garrison still went on his way with a brave heart. "Our cause is of God," he answered, "and we need not fear the results of conflict." And still it was his aim by moral influence alone to awaken the consciences of the people of the Northern States, and to rouse public opinion against the great sin that brought the North its wealth.

In old times men suffered martyrdom as heretics for holding beliefs that in the next age were held as sacred truths by the children of the persecutors. "Slowly the Bible of the race is writ." William Lloyd Garrison, bearing patiently the hard names of atheist and unbeliever, was teaching his fellow-countrymen other lessons besides the evil of slavery. He was showing them, though they were slow to learn, that Christianity does not consist in creeds and forms, but in a life of loving service; that God's word is not confined to the pages of a book, however grand that book may be, but is still spoken every day in the consciences of men who will listen to His whisper with open ears.

CHAPTER IX.

"*NO UNION WITH SLAVE-HOLDERS!*"

O the west of the busy cities of the United States lay vast territories stretching out to the foot of the Rocky Mountains. The fresh winds swept over their prairies and forests, and the sun rose and set over the broad uncultivated land, which, as yet, few civilized men had ever looked upon. The slave-holders of the Southern States who wanted to extend the slave trade began to turn their gaze towards those unclaimed territories, and, when plans were made for adding them as new States to the Union, resolved at all costs to establish slavery in them.

Texas, one of those great outlying lands, really belonged to Mexico. But popular opinion said, "Might is Right," and in the

year 1845 the United States went to war
with Mexico, and in the end a part of
Texas was added to the slave States. Still,
Kansas and Nebraska lay outside the Union.
On their borderland lived peaceful, happy
settlers, farming their plots of ground and
hating slavery with all their hearts. The
time was coming when these territories would
be also added to the United States; and the
question was still unanswered, would the slave-
power gain these dominions, or would they
be joined to the number of the free States of
the North? William Lloyd Garrison, always
watchful and alert, discovered the slave-holders'
plot. He saw that if they gained their way
in these territories, they would not only extend
their slave trade—they would also increase their
representation in Congress. Already most of
the laws passed by the United States Government favoured slavery. One fact became
more and more clear to him—the free North
could not rightly carry out these laws, and the
union of the free and slave States must be
broken!

Think what courage was needed to make
this statement. The Union was the idol

of every American. It was no less than treason to the State to suggest the breaking of this bond. No other newspaper editor dared to utter such a thought. Yet this was the new word that Garrison felt called upon to speak; and forth from the *Liberator* came the clear tones : " This criminal Union must be broken. The free North must have no union with slave-holders. There must be no delay—the bond between the North and South must be severed." Garrison did not stop to ask, "What will become of me if I make this declaration?"—not even "What will my friends say?" His only thought was, "What is right?" And once more as in old days he said to himself, "I am in earnest. I will not equivocate. I will not retreat a single inch : and *I will be heard.*" It was true division had weakened his cause. No matter, right is right, and if he had stood quite alone, he would still have set himself the task of wakening the con-science of his fellow-men to see that they must have no union with oppressors.

When Garrison had been for some months writing in this bold tone in the *Liberator*, a new voice began to make itself heard in

Boston. Early in 1845, Theodore Parker was preaching in the Melodeon—a large hall in the city. He had come to Boston from West Roxbury, a quiet country village not many miles away. There farmers had been his hearers in the little church among the fields. Now, out of back streets and city slums came the hard-worked, weary men and women to listen to the preacher whose words brought a living religion and a new spring of hope into their dark lives. And the secret of this man's power was that from boyhood he had listened to the whispers of his conscience, and believed that the living God speaks *now* in the conscience of every man, woman, and child as plainly as ever He spoke to prophets in the days of old. So the message he had to give he always gave with vigour and earnestness; and when, very soon after his arrival in Boston, he met with Garrison, he found that he must use his influence with the great crowds that flocked to hear him in the Melodeon, to teach them that there was a " higher law," which forbade the slavery legalized by the laws of the United States. Then, while most other preachers did not dare to speak on the subject, he "thundered" against slavery, and it was not long before he had to help Garrison in work as well as in words.

One day a ship from New Orleans, in the Southern States, sailed into Boston harbour. She was owned by Boston merchants, and manned by Boston sailors. Unknown to captain and crew, a slave at New Orleans had managed to escape from his owner, while the ship still lay in the dock, and had hidden himself away among the merchandise in the dark hold. At the end of the voyage, when the vessel was moored in Boston harbour, the poor stowaway crawled from his hiding-place, hoping to find himself at last a free man in this city of the free States, where no slaves were ever bought or sold. Great was the excitement in Boston when the owners of the ship sent the miserable man back to his master in New Orleans; and there was no law but the moral law, which they did not heed, to say them nay. At once Garrison and Theodore Parker joined together to summon a great meeting in Faneuil Hall. The crowd gathered round the doors long before they were opened, and it is said the hall was packed from floor to roof. At that meeting a vigilance committee was formed of well-known anti-slavery workers who bound themselves to prevent the repetition of such an outrage in the city.

But not alone in Boston were the friends of freedom roused by deeds of cruelty and wrong, which took place on the free soil of the Northern States. Such events multiplied as the anti-slavery struggle deepened. In 1850 a new law was passed in Congress, and the tidings spread quickly through the land that by this " *Fugitive Slave Bill* " the law of the land had decreed heavy fine and imprisonment for any person in the Northern States who gave shelter to a slave escaped from his owner in the South. Kidnappers and spies sped on their cruel errands from town to town, and the miserable fugitives were hunted and tracked and carried back to bondage. Not only so, the children of freed negroes who had never been in slavery were seized and taken captive to the slave States. No coloured person was from that time safe anywhere in the United States.

But if tales of horror are told of those days, there are grand stories also to tell of the heroism of men and women who feared no danger that might result to themselves, and bravely sheltered and rescued the persecuted slaves. Boston Court-house was hung with chains; the slave pens were filled with miserable fugitives; but Garrison and Theodore Parker used to make their way there, and speak hopeful, comforting words to the poor trembling prisoners; and it was well known in Boston that neither of these two men would scruple to break this new infamous Fugitive Slave Law.

The year 1850, and many years that followed, were marked by shameful compromises and weak yielding for the sake of peace on the part of the Northern States. Again and again did they give way to the demands of the slave-holding South. In those times Garrison's voice was always clear. He never faltered, never gave way when enemies tried to bribe and threaten him. "This criminal union with slave-holders must be broken," was still his cry. No wonder that with his whole honest soul he hated those compromising times. In

1854, another famous measure was passed by vote of Congress. It was known by the name of the "Kansas Nebraska Bill," and at the same time the "Missouri Compromise," dating from the year 1820, which prohibited the extension of slavery north and west of the State of Missouri, was repealed; for this new law decreed that the inhabitants of the great western territories should decide for themselves by vote the question of admitting slavery within their borders, and both Kansas and Nebraska lay beyond that boundary fixed by the Missouri Compromise more than thirty years before. Nor did the plotting of the Southern States end here. The voting in Kansas and Nebraska must be managed so that the slave system should gain the day; and a host of "border ruffians" from the South poured in upon the peaceful farmers settled there, and plundered and burned their homes, with the design of driving away those old dwellers who would vote against the establishment of slavery in their midst. But an unexpected result followed. Not for the sake of freedom, buf to help the plundered settlers, the Northern States sent down men and arms to Kansas, and a kind of civil war broke out that lasted many a weary year.

Like a great rock firmly planted amid shifting sands or storm-beaten waters, William Lloyd Garrison stands out among the fickle, time-serving politicians of those days. True to his early aim of rousing the moral indignation of the people against slavery, he would have nothing to do with the political aspect of the question. "Waken the consciences of the people," he said, " and the laws will be mended." So on this point he was contented once more to stand almost alone, and part company from his friends, who could not see with him that to exercise the right of voting even was one way of supporting a criminal Government. It is not a matter for debate, in this short story of Garrison's life, whether ho or his friends were right in this matter. His conscience told him that he must have no dealings with the " unclean thing," and he also feared that hope of fame or popular applause might lower the aim of men who tried to work for the anti-slavery cause by any *political* channel. Always at the head of the great *moral* movement stood this American hero, crying, " Right is right, and the free North must have no dealings with the slave-holders of the South." Again and again all would have been lost in those years of hesitation and compromise on the part of the United States Government, but for Garrison and men like him who stood firm to principle, and would not equivocate or retreat an inch.

The passing of the Fugitive Slave Bill in 1850 had startled many careless souls who thought little of the sorrows of the kidnapped slaves before the Act was passed which *legalized* his capture. A still greater shock was felt when the judgment was passed in the Supreme Court of the United States that the " negro had no rights which a white man need regard." Surely Garrison's constant warnings against the iniquity of the laws framed by the Union were borne out by facts. Politicians began to study the *Liberator*, and lectures given by Garrison, Wendell Phillips, S. J. May, Theodore Parker, and many other anti-slavery orators, were crowded by eager listeners. Frederick Douglas, too, a noble coloured man who had tasted the horrors of slavery himself, had joined the band of workers, and was giving up life and strength to help his kindred still in chains. Whittier was pouring forth fresh "Songs of Freedom," and his verses rang through the land as each new occasion for shame or triumph rose.

So the chorus of voices swelled and deepened, and the year 1860 drew near. As beacon fires answer each other from the mountain tops, so the indignant protests against the encroachments of the Southern slave power were heard in one State after another, and the answer came back from the far-away west. The crisis was at hand, and England, watching from across the sea, recalled her own great struggle, and knew that in some way the victory was about to be won.

CHAPTER X.

THE TRIUMPH OF THE RIGHT.

IN the days when William Lloyd Garrison was yet a little lad running errands for his master about the hilly streets of Newburyport, another boy, whose name was destined to be as famous in the history of the anti-slavery struggle, was spending his youth among settlers in the waste lands of Indiana. A rough log cabin was his home, and his growing strength was used in helping his father to cut down the forest trees, to pile the timber up, and cultivate the land they cleared with so much labour. It was very rare to find among those toil-worn settlers any love of letters; yet this boy might be seen, when work was over, teaching himself to write by the light of the log fire, and patiently making letters with a charred stick on a rough wooden board. A Bible, catechism, and spelling book had descended to his family from more prosperous days, and the young student pored over them, and kept this treasured library safe from wind and rain under the eaves of the wooden roof.

By-and-by fresh emigrants settled in the neighbourhood, and new interests came into the narrow round of the log-cabin life. Years afterwards, Abraham Lincoln—for so the boy was called—-remembered the eagerness with which he had walked many miles to borrow a life of Washington from one of those new-comers; the grief with which he found the volume, in its hiding-place under the roof, soaked by a storm that had risen in the night; and the willingness with which he worked for its owner until he had paid the worth of the damaged book, and made the Life of Washington his own.

As he grew older, Abraham became known for his dry humour. His quaint sayings and odd jokes made the forest-clearers merry as they sat and rested from their work. It was a common thing for him to mount the stump

of a tree in the harvest field, and there repeat
long passages to the reapers from the few
books he had read, or make a speech in rough,
but telling words, careless whether he had few
or many hearers. But there was another side
to this young orator's character. Behind the
jokes lay a vein of sadness; behind the rough
outside a tender heart, well known to his
father, step-mother, and sister, and the close
companions of his life. Abraham Lincoln was
never known to be anything but gentle to
either man or beast; and whether he hired
himself out, or worked with his father cutting
timber in the forest, or paddled the flat boat
which he had built to carry produce to the
nearest market down the river, he was always
ready to give a helping hand to any one who
needed it.

Time passed, and new plans were formed
by the Lincoln household. Abraham's father
resolved to leave the rough log cabin in
Indiana, and settle two hundred miles away
in the State of Illinois. Strange day-dreams
had been visiting young Lincoln's mind of
late—visions of other work than forest-clear-
ing; and as he walked by the side of the great

wagon that carried the household goods to the
new home, his thoughts went out towards the
wide, unknown world which lay before his
opening manhood. But he would not leave
his father till he saw him well settled, and the
strong, capable young man had no difficulty in
getting work with the farmers of Illinois. So
he split rails all day to pay for his food and
clothing, and walked six or seven miles night
and morning to the various farms, reading as
he went on his way, whenever he was fortunate
enough to have the rare treat of a borrowed
book.

In the winter of 1830 an offer was made to
him to take part charge of a boat-load of pork
and corn down the river Mississippi to New
Orleans. Then he had his first glimpse of the
horrors of slavery, and the sights in New
Orleans he never forgot. The cargo was well
sold, and a better offer followed. A store-
keeper was wanted at the little settlement of
New Salem, in Illinois, and Abraham Lincoln
was chosen for the post. Because he could
read and write—rare accomplishments in that
region—he was made clerk at the polling booth
during an election there, and he became well

K

known all over that part of the country. Now he began to read a newspaper regularly, and to interest himself in the politics of the times. The poor settlers looked upon him as a wise councillor, and they made him umpire and peacemaker in their quarrels. He was known everywhere as "Honest Abe," and welcomed in every log cabin and village home that he entered. It was said that he was "the best-natured, best-informed, most modest, kindest, gentlest, roughest, strongest, best young fellow in all New Salem and the region round about."

Perhaps those uncultivated, hard-working settlers valued most, of all young Lincoln's qualities, his physical courage and great bodily powers. They made him captain of a volunteer band, and he led his men out against "Black Hawk," an Indian chief who was making inroads on the white men's settlements. They were all proud of him for his great strength of arm. The marvels of his rail-chopping and harvest work passed from mouth to mouth quite as readily as did his exploits as a man of letters or an arbitrator. And this strength was used so often and so

helpfully for weaker men, that the anecdotes
told of him read like tales of the feats of some
good genius who set himself the task of clear-
ing obstacles and troubles from the pathway of
heavily laden mortals.

Step by step new chances opened out before
Abraham Lincoln, and he used them wisely.
He was made postmaster of New Salem, and
gained more influence in consequence. Picture
him reading the newspaper, and commenting
on its politics to the little crowd gathered at
evening round the entrance to his store. Many
poor hearts were cheered in those days when
the good postmaster deciphered to them the
precious ill-spelt letters which they could not
read from dear ones far away from the old
home. At length he was asked to offer himself as candidate for the Illinois Legislature.
He lost the election, for he was true to principles which were not popular ; but he was
still " Honest Abe," and on the next trial his
candidature was successful. No one who
knew Abraham's tender, honest heart, wondered to hear that from his place in the State
House he protested again and again against
resolutions in favour of slavery. For eight

years he was a member at intervals of the Illinois Legislature ; then a higher honour was conferred on him, and for one term he was elected as member for that State to the House of Representatives in Washington, where he made many vigorous speeches against the war with Mexico and the annexation of Texas as a slave state. So he became known throughout the country as an anti-slavery legislator.

Meanwhile, he had studied for the law, and entered into partnership with a well-known lawyer at Springfield, in Illinois, and became successful in his profession, and famous, too, for his honesty and his generous help of clients who were too poor ever to repay his services. He had not sought re-election to the House of Representatives, and the days came when the struggle in Kansas arose, and when the en-croachments of the Southern slave power over the yielding North were increasing rapidly. "Honest Abe" burnt with indignation, and more than once he canvassed the States as a candidate for the Senate. Not disheartened by failure, he travelled from town to town to lecture, and his popularity was very great. As he watched the signs of the times, he saw that the struggle was gradually absorbing the life of the nation, and that without doubt the end was drawing nigh.

When the year 1860 opened, a great event was at hand. Before the close of the coming twelve months, a new President would have been chosen to rule over the people of the United States.

Would he be in favour of freedom or slavery? What would the voters of the great nation decree? How far had public opinion been moved by the events of the past few years, and the labours of William Lloyd Garrison and the workers who had risen up around him? In May, the people of Illinois chose Abraham Lincoln for their candidate. Six months must pass before the election, and the wildest excitement spread through the land. On the 6th of November, 1860, Abraham Lincoln was declared sixteenth President of the United States, and the thirty millions of people who were his fellow-countrymen heard the news with very varied feelings.

Lincoln was known as an Abolitionist, and the Southerners saw an end to their hopes of extending slavery. He entered office March

4th, 1861, and having bound himself to preserve the Union, he did all in his power as President to uphold friendly relations with the South; but on one point he was firm—slavery should *not* increase further on the free lands of the North and West. Garrison, with his resolute mind fixed on immediate abolition, on *no* delay in doing right, distrusted the new President's measures; but the day came when Abraham Lincoln was found to be firm as a rock, when South Carolina summoned a State Convention at Charleston, the Southern States seceded, and the first shot of the rebellion was fired from Fort Sumter in Charleston Harbour.

Garrison saw now that slavery was doomed to perish. The great uprising of the Northern States to suppress the rebellion had changed the aspect of affairs. Events followed one another in quick succession. The Northern senators withstood the slave-holders boldly in the Senate House, and the terrible war swept over the country. All might have been prevented if enough men like Garrison had been true to the right from the first. Garrison was a man of peace, and this war which he had dreaded was a fearful ending to the slavery he had so long been struggling against. But the end had come, and his advice to the Northern soldiers was, "You believe in war—then do your duty and fight for the right."

At last the great proclamation was issued by the President which promised freedom to every slave in the rebel States on the first day in the year 1863. *Then* Garrison believed in Abraham Lincoln, and more than one conference took place between the two men who now acknowledged the same end and aim. And so four million slaves were at last free men; but the President knew and felt that the great moral influence exercised in past years by Garrison was the real source of the triumph he had stepped in to win.

This is no history of the war. As an episode in Garrison's stormy life, it enters into this story; but there is no space and no need to tell of the awful battle-fields, and the desolate homes, and the fierce struggle of relatives and friends who met in hand-to-hand conflict during this appalling civil war. It lasted four long years. On April 9th, 1865, the commander of the Confederate army, General Lee, surrendered, and there was peace in the land. By Act of

Congress, every one throughout the nation was declared free for evermore. The glad news was rung out in the country, and amid the roaring of cannon and the rejoicings of the people, it was proclaimed that war and slavery were at an end.

John Greenleaf Whittier, the poet of the people, faithful to the last to the anti-slavery work for which Garrison had summoned him from his paradise at Haverhill, wrote more than one song of thanksgiving that year. Probably his " Peace Autumn," some verses of which follow, spoke in poets' language the thoughts of many hearts :—

" Thank God for rest, where none molest,
    And none can make afraid ;
For peace that sits as plenty's guest
    Beneath the homestead shade.

" Bring pike and gun, the sword's red scourge,
    The negro's broken chains,
And beat them at the blacksmith's forge
    To ploughshares for our plains.

" Alike henceforth our hills of snow,
    And vales where cotton flowers :
All streams that flow, all winds that blow,
    Are freedom's motive powers.

" Build up an altar to the Lord,
  Oh grateful hearts of ours !
And shape it of the greenest sward
  That ever drank the showers.

" Lay all the bloom of gardens there,
  And there the orchard fruits ;
Bring golden grain from sun and air,
  From earth her goodly roots.

" There let our banners droop and flow,
  The stars uprise and fall ;
Our roll of martyrs, sad and slow,
  Let sighing breezes call.

" Their names let hands of horn and tan
  And rough-shod feet applaud,
Who died to make the slave a man,
  And link with toil reward.

" There let the common heart keep time,
  To such an anthem sung
As never swelled on poet's rhyme,
  Or thrilled on singer's tongue.

" A song of faith that trusts the end
  To match the good begun ;
Nor doubts the power of love to blend
  The hearts of men as one."

And thus the great struggle to which William
Lloyd Garrison had consecrated his life was
over. " Thank God," he said, " I am an
Abolitionist no longer." The American Anti-

Slavery Society was dissolved, and the publication of the *Liberator* ceased. Thirty-five years had passed since the first number made its way down into the Boston streets from the poor, gloomy garret in which the " mad-cap Garrison " had begun his apparently hopeless task.

One day before the close of that memorable year 1865, Garrison received an official invitation to the city of Charleston, in South Carolina. The flag of the Union was to be raised again among great rejoicings on Fort Sumter, whence the first shot in the rebellion had been fired. His friend, George Thompson, who had shared some of his dangers in past years, was again in America, and accompanied him, for he, too, was to be an honoured guest of the Government. The English orator, who had seen the victory of hard-won causes in his own land, bore home with him undying memories of that visit to the city that had so lately been in the centre of the slave-system.

" I am going," he wrote to a friend, " to celebrate the triumph of Garrisonian abolitionism in Charleston—going in company with Garrison himself."

And such a triumph was celebrated there as

Charleston never saw before, and probably will never see again. From early morning, songs of joy and shouts of welcome resounded; the streets were filled with vast hosts of freed men, who thronged round Garrison, and bore him on their shoulders, and could not find means to testify the gratitude they felt. Later in the day a great gathering was held in the largest church in the city. Three thousand freed negroes met together in the building, and Garrison received a wreath of flowers from the hands of children who had been slaves only a year before. Speeches were made by the freed men, and by the visitors who had come to Charleston to the celebration, and all joined to honour Garrison, who not long before had been an outlaw in the South. Meanwhile his thoughts turned to the friends and helpers who had also worked so bravely during the struggle. Perhaps the form of the brave old Quaker, Benjamin Lundy, rose, in fancy, before him; and of Isaac Knapp, the friend of his youth; of the good merchant, Arthur Tappan, and the poet Whittier; of the Rev. S. J. May; of brave Prudence Crandall, and the noble women of Philadelphia, Boston, and New

York; of Theodore Parker and Wendell Phillips, and a host of others. However that might be, in the fashion of all true heroes, he gave the glory of the victory to his comrades in the work, and in his reply he spoke of George Thompson's valiant labours in the cause, and did honour to senators and politicians who had laboured in later years for the slaves, though on lines differing from his own. And whenever Abraham Lincoln's name was heard that day, it is said that the cheers of the people sounded " like the roaring of the sea in storm."

Two years later Mr. Garrison paid a visit to England. Soon after his arrival, noted men of all creeds and varied politics met together in St. James's Hall, in London, to do honour to the American hero. Some of the words he spoke on that occasion fitly illustrate the spirit of his life.

"I must here disclaim," he said, " with all sincerity of soul, any special praise for anything I have done. I have simply tried to maintain the integrity of my soul before God and to do my duty. I have refused to go with the multitude to do evil. I have endeavoured to save my country from crime. I have sought to liberate such as were held captive in the house of bondage. But all this I ought to have done. Henceforth, through all coming time, advocates of justice and friends of reform, be not discouraged; for you will and you must succeed if you have a righteous cause. No matter at the outset how few may be disposed to rally round the standard you have raised, if you battle unflinchingly and without compromise, if yours is the faith that cannot be shaken, because it is linked to the eternal throne, it is only a question of time when victory shall come to reward your toils. So it has been, so it is, so it ever will be throughout the earth in any conflict for the right!"

CHAPTER XI.

SUNSET.

"THEY cannot reach up to the level of my home mood." In these words Mr. Garrison often spoke of the heavy cares and perplexities that made up so much of his life during the long anti-slavery struggle. An old friend says of him, "He was always courageous and hopeful. Never in a single instance did I see him in a discouraged mood. His faith in the goodness of his cause, and in the over-ruling providence of God, was so absolute that he was calm and cheerful alike under clear and cloudy skies. I have seen him again and again, when the expenses of the *Liberator* were running far beyond its receipts, and he did not know whence the money was to come to supply the wants of his family; but never once did

any shadow fall on his spirit on this account.
He had given himself and all his powers to a
cause that he believed had the favour and
support of Heaven, and he did not doubt that
he would be taken care of." *

And now that the struggle was over, its
leader was a man of sixty years of age—in
broken health—who had spent his strength and
all the best days of his life in the service of
humanity. And though he wished for no other
reward than the triumph of the cause for
which he had worked, his grateful country
desired that her hero's closing years should be
passed in peace and sunshine.

So his friends in America and across the sea
in England joined together to subscribe the
sum of thirty thousand dollars, that no further
anxieties as to the support of his family might
press upon him. And at Roxbury, where he
and his young wife had begun their married
life in " Freedom's Cottage," he bought a
pleasant country house called " Rockledge."
Old friends loved to visit this happy home, and
to talk over the days that, as Garrison said,

* " William Lloyd Garrison and his Times," by Oliver
Johnson, p. 396.

"had tried men's souls," and new friends found a genial welcome there, and carried sacred memories away. Mr. Garrison had five children living: two of them had reached man's estate, and were doing their own good work in the world. In course of time, his only daughter married and went to New York; but both sons and daughter often came back to "Rockledge," and the merry voices of little grandchildren gave an added brightness to the house.

There was scarcely a shadow cast on this brightness when Mrs. Garrison, the faithful wife and mother, became an invalid; for her cheerfulness and sunny ways made every one about her glad, and brought out all the tenderness which formed so large a part of Mr. Garrison's character. And still he found time to work for the world, and took up the great questions of temperance and peace, and women's work, and purity in social life, and his wonderful influence made itself widely felt, though most of his days were passed in the retirement of his country home.

In 1876 his wife died. The following year he went to England with one of his sons. Declining all public receptions, he spent three

months in wandering through beautiful scenery,
and in quiet visits to old friends. He never
crossed the Atlantic again, and many warm
English hearts treasured his parting words as
he took leave of all in the old country: "If
we do not meet again in this world, we surely
shall in a better."

After this journey, his health became gradually more infirm, and towards the end of the
year 1878 he began, both in his letters and his
conversation, to speak of "going home."
When staying with his daughter, Mrs. Villard,
at New York, in the following spring, the summons came. He passed away peacefully in the
midst of his children and grandchildren as they
sang to him his favourite hymns, and the world
heard with sorrow, on May 24th, 1879, that
William Lloyd Garrison was dead.

The story of his funeral has no gloom about
it. The lifeless body was carried back to
"Rockledge," and on May 28th, when the
neighbouring church was filled with sunlight
and bright with flowers, his family and a large
assemblage of people gathered together there,
and looked for the last time on the face of
their friend. John Greenleaf Whittier wrote a

L

farewell poem, which was read on the occasion, and addresses were delivered by Wendell Phillips and other old friends and fellow-workers.

There is a beautiful cemetery, called "Forest Hills," near Roxbury. There William Lloyd Garrison was laid beside his wife, while the sky was glowing with the colours of the sunset, and round the grave coloured men and women sang a parting hymn.

And so the story of an American hero ends. It tells of a mighty movement which gave freedom in the end to four millions of slaves, and owed its birth to a poor, self-taught printer-boy, who vowed to be true to the right though the whole world was against him.

www.ingramcontent.com/pod-product-compliance
Lightning Source LLC
Chambersburg PA
CBHW030901050726
47500CB00009B/847